Talia Talk

ALSO BY CHRISTINE HURLEY DERISO

The Right-Under Club
Do-Over

Talia Talk

CHRISTINE HURLEY DERISO

Delacorte Press

Published by Delacorte Press
an imprint of Random House Children's Books
a division of Random House, Inc.
New York

Visit us on the Web! www.randomhouse.com/kids

Educators and librarians, for a variety of teaching tools, visit us at
www.randomhouse.com/teachers

Library of Congress Cataloging-in-Publication Data
Deriso, Christine Hurley.
Talia Talk / Christine Hurley Deriso. — 1st ed.
p. cm.
Summary: Trying to fit in despite having a loud, embarrassing best friend,
eleven-year-old Talia becomes a commentator on her middle school's closed-
circuit television program and turns the tables on her mother, a talk show host
who has been revealing Talia's most humiliating experiences for years.
ISBN: 978-0-385-73620-6 (hardcover)—ISBN: 978-0-385-90592-3 (lib. bdg.)
ISBN: 978-0-375-84496-6 (pbk.)
[1. Best friends—Fiction. 2. Friendship—Fiction. 3. Television talk shows—
Fiction. 4. Celebrities—Fiction. 5. Middle schools—Fiction. 6. Schools—
Fiction. 7. Mothers and daughters—Fiction. 8. Single-parent
families—Fiction.] I. Title.
PZ7.D4427Tal 2009
[Fic]—dc22
2007050556

The text of this book is set in 12-point Goudy.

Book design by Kenny Holcomb

Printed in the United States of America

10 9 8 7 6 5 4 3 2 1

First Edition

To Greg, with all my love.
Don't forget our deal.

1

"Pull, Otters, pull!"

I squinted and puffed out my cheeks. Weighing only about ninety-eight pounds, I didn't have much to offer my team besides fierce facial expressions. Plus, my hands were sore by now, so maybe my squinting would fool people into thinking I was actually trying.

"Harder, Talia, harder!"

Busted. My best friend, Bridget, was at the front of our team's line (Bridget had been in front of every line I'd ever been in), but even with me standing behind her, she could tell my heart wasn't in it. Tug-of-war was totally pointless.

But not to Bridget. Bridget was so competitive, she could turn a spelling bee into a contact sport. And tug-of-war against a team that included Meredith and Brynne? The

1

rope might as well have been a red cape flashing in front of a bull. Bridget would own that rope, even if she had to pull five times as hard to compensate for her scrawny teammates (me being the scrawniest and, let's face it, the least motivated). To Bridget, it was a matter of principle . . . of willpower . . . of sheer determination. That, and since she was at the front of the line, she'd be the one to tumble into the muddy creek if we lost.

Through my squint, I noticed Meredith and Brynne pulling on the opposite side of the creek bank. Even in the middle of tug-of-war, their ponytails looked bouncy and their lips glossy. What was it with those two? When had they morphed from scabby-kneed goofballs to dainty princesses? And why hadn't Bridget and I received the morph memo?

"*Pull harder, Otters!*" Bridget bellowed, clutching the rope with one hand while she quickly wiped the sweat from her brow with the other.

Which was all it took for Meredith and Brynne's team to give the final heave that knocked Bridget off balance and sent her tumbling into the creek. My fellow Otters and I groaned gamely but didn't exactly have rope burns on our hands.

The camp counselor blew a whistle. "Game, Sea Turtles," she said in a last-day-of-camp monotone before adjusting the score on a clipboard.

Meredith and Brynne pointed at Bridget thrashing in the ankle-deep creek water and giggled into their fingertips. They dropped the rope and gave each other high fives, then turned to their teammates for more palm slapping.

"Sea Turtles rule!" Meredith crowed, which, let's face it, was the understatement of the millennium. If there had been any doubt at the beginning of the week that the Sea Turtles ruled, by the last day of camp, we were all clear.

"Weaklings!" Bridget moaned as she staggered to her feet and splashed us with creek water. "We've lost almost every single competition this week!"

My fellow Otters and I nodded apologetically but couldn't help sucking in our own giggles. Bridget was covered in mud and looked like she might spin off into space, her head was shaking so indignantly.

"It's just a game, Bridge," I said.

"*Just a game!*" she roared. I might as well have said "just a nuclear war."

Meredith and Brynne nonchalantly inspected their nails and tightened their ponytails.

"So what's the damage for the week?" Meredith asked our counselor.

The counselor tapped items on the clipboard, counting as she went along. "Sea Turtles ten, Otters one."

"Well . . . our quilt is prettier!" I sputtered, then thought that might possibly be the lamest thing I'd ever said.

"Maybe you girls better stick to quilting," Brynne said, rubbing her hands on the back of her jean shorts. She and Meredith waved a fluttery goodbye, then headed back toward the mess hall for lunch.

The counselor and other campers scattered too, except for me. Bridget had crumpled in defeat back onto the creek bank, and I sat beside her for moral support, ignoring the mud creeping up my thighs.

"Don't utter a word about camp to my mom," I said, planting my chin in my hand. "I can see it now: she'll yak on her show about how hopeless we were in every competition except quilting, and the whole town will send me fabric patches to try to cheer me up."

Mom's TV fame had started innocently enough. After my dad died of cancer when I was seven, she got a job doing the morning news for WBJM. Sitting behind a shiny oak desk and reading off a TelePrompTer, she told viewers about local elections, courtroom verdicts, traffic snags and other items that fall under the category "Things I Don't Mind the World Knowing About."

But she was such a hit on the news that, pretty soon, her producer asked her to cohost WBJM's chatty midmorning show, *Up and At 'Em*, an hourlong hodgepodge of host chat, interviews and artsy-craftsy segments. Host chat usually covers items that fall under the category of "Things I Mind the World Knowing About." Things like how I threw up on my piano teacher while she played a duet with me during a recital. It was tough enough being a kid (and a half-orphan at that) without everybody in town knowing about my intestinal woes.

Viewers always raved about how funny and charming my mom was. Whatever. It never struck me as funny or charming that the whole town knew I had a first-grade crush on the paperboy and just happened to be "dusting the porch" every time he came by. Why did anyone else need to know about the time I trick-or-treated as a road map because I'd used a permanent marker to connect the dots of my chicken pox? And whose business was it that I glued antlers onto my head with bubble gum one Christmas?

Trying *not* to watch my mom's humiliating tell-alls was like trying *not* to think about a polka-dot elephant when somebody says "No matter what you do, don't think about a polka-dot elephant." Just knowing I was being talked about was excruciating enough. Knowing without knowing the specifics was even worse and drove my imagination into overdrive.

"Promise me," I said to Bridget, "if Mom asks how camp was, just say fine."

Bridget shrugged. "It's not the worst thing in the world to have a mom who's a celebrity," she said. "Being the kid of a teacher is worse." Bridget was so sure of herself that when she offered an opinion, she sounded like she was reading from a history book: "*When the pilgrims landed at Plymouth Rock, they encountered Native Americans, who introduced them to maize and explained to them that being the kid of a teacher is worse than being the kid of a celebrity.*"

"No way," I said.

"Way."

"Prove it, Smarty Pants," I told her. "Compare and contrast."

Bridget smiled, like she'd studied the subject and had been waiting for someone to ask. "Your mom can tell the whole town about your rashes," she said, making me cringe with the reminder that, yes, Mom had recently gabbed about my rash. "But *my* mom," she continued slowly, raising her eyebrows, "is like a walking billboard: 'My kid is doomed.' "

"Not as doomed as me," I grumbled.

" '*I*,' " Bridget said. " 'Not as doomed as *I*.' "

I narrowed my eyes. "What are you, my English teacher?"

"See? Teachers really *are* annoying."

"But even teachers don't blab their kids' secrets all over town," I pointed out. "And we'll be in middle school in the fall, so you won't be in your mom's school anymore."

Bridget considered this for a moment, then said, "Well, your mom could be the lunch lady and make you eat left-over school mush every day for dinner. *That* would be worse than having a celebrity for a mom."

And I really couldn't argue with that.

Bridget pulled a wildflower from the ground and absently plucked its petals. "Camp used to be so fun," she said.

"That's when Mer and Brynne used to be fun," I said. "Now, they're just . . . fungus."

Bridget looked at me quizzically and I shrugged. It was the best insult I could muster off the top of my head.

Funny how Bridget and I had suddenly found ourselves on the outs with Mer and Brynne. Until recently, the four of us had been inseparable—playing kickball in my front yard, building a fort in the woods behind Bridget's house, inventing new Pop-Tart-based desserts in Brynne's kitchen, trimming each other's bangs in Meredith's froufrou bedroom. . . . It was at the beginning of summer that Meredith and Brynne had started making up excuses not to join us on the trampoline or race through our path in the woods. But even then, we still felt like a foursome.

Until camp. They'd acted like they were allergic to us

6

from day one, and Bridget writhing in the mud on our last day symbolized the slow death of our friendship.

Mer and Brynne had killed it.

● ● ●

"So I guess I'll see you when school starts next week."

I folded a T-shirt and stuffed it into my duffel bag as Brynne and I packed side by side. Our cots were adjacent in the cabin, but this summer, we'd forgone our usual camp tradition of whispering secrets till three in the morning. The best we'd been able to manage this week was tight smiles as we made our beds, then crisp "good nights" before lights out. Things were even icier at the other end of the cabin, where Bridget's and Meredith's cots were.

"Yeah. Guess I'll see you then," Brynne responded without looking up from the jeans she was folding.

I sighed and let a pair of underwear drop from my fingers. I took a couple of seconds to gather my courage, then planted my hands on my hips and looked straight at Brynne.

"Why aren't we friends anymore?" I asked softly.

Brynne's eyelashes fluttered. At first, she tried to keep her gaze planted on her duffel, but after a moment, her green eyes locked with mine.

"It's Bridget," she said, the words tumbling out as if they'd been held captive in her mouth all week. "She's so loud. And bossy."

"She's always been loud and bossy," I replied, feeling a little guilty, but, hey, that wasn't exactly a news flash, was it?

"Uh, duh," Brynne said, as if I'd just proved her point.

"And obnoxious. Did you notice how she was stamping on everybody's feet during the hoedown? And playing pool with her French fries and peas in the mess hall? When I came out of the shower last night, she'd hung my pajamas from a tree and left a Barbie outfit on my cot in their place. I had to go outside in my towel to get my pj's! And did you hear she filled Meredith's shampoo bottle with syrup? God. She is so immature."

I frowned. "But we've all been best friends since kindergarten."

Brynne's fingernails dug into her jeans. "We're not in kindergarten anymore," she said. "Bridget embarrasses us."

Right. "Us." She and Mer were now definitely an "us." Apparently, so were Bridget and I, since I was somehow being held responsible for her being loud and obnoxious.

"Bridget's a great friend," I said defensively. "Who ran five blocks to get your mom when you broke your nose skating?"

Brynne shook her head slowly—a "you just don't understand" head shake. "We're in middle school now," she said, as if that explained it all. "But we miss you, Talia. Meredith's sleeping over tomorrow night. Why don't you come?"

My eyebrows arched. "We all sleep over at Bridget's house the night after camp. It's a tradition."

How stupid. After the way this week had gone, it would take a total moron not to realize our tradition was history.

"Can we at least hang out in school?" I asked pleadingly.

Brynne stared at her hands. "Yeah. I'm sure we'll see each other around. It's just . . ."

She didn't finish her sentence.

She didn't have to.

It was happening again.

The look.

My mom and I had stopped by the grocery store on the way home from camp. We were squeezing cantaloupes in the produce section—well, *she* was squeezing cantaloupes and I was inspecting my split ends—when I remembered why I should never inspect my split ends in public.

The lady in the produce aisle glanced right past us at first. But then her eyes widened, and then her eyelashes fluttered as she forced herself to look away. Next came the pause, then the sneak-peek back at Mom.

"You're Chelsea from *Up and At 'Em!*" Tomato Lady said, holding her bag of produce in one hand and pointing at Mom with the other. She was already walking toward us.

"Guilty as charged," Mom said. That's what she always

said when she was recognized, and always in that "I'm humble and a good sport" kind of way. Next, she would toss me a sympathy glance and we'd steel ourselves for a ten-minute conversation with a complete stranger.

"Oh, I love your show!" Tomato Lady gushed. "You're so witty! I watch you every morning, and you always make me laugh." Pause as Tomato Lady's eyes moved from Mom to me. "And you must be Talia!"

Pinch alert! Pinch alert!

I managed to smile back, but it was my fake smile, the kind that didn't make it all the way up to my eyes.

"I laughed for half an hour straight when your mom talked about you throwing up on your piano teacher's shoes at your recital!" Tomato Lady told me.

"Oh, that was *ages* ago," Mom said, trying to soften the blow, but Tomato Lady might as well have smacked me in the face with a piece of produce.

"I don't blame you for being nervous, dear," Tomato Lady said, and here it came: the face pinch. *Grrrrr* . . . "I used to give piano lessons myself, and I know how the tummy fills with butterflies on the big day. Of course, I never had a student throw up on me—"

"Well, that's all behind her now," Mom said too quickly. "She's blossoming into a beautiful young woman."

Tomato Lady studied me with a crinkled brow, trying for the life of her to see the beautiful young woman in my gangly eleven-year-old body clad in mud-stained shorts. Didn't Mom know by now that her lame remarks only made things worse?

"Right," Tomato Lady said, unconvinced, but then her face brightened again. "I feel like I know you, Talia!"

"Oh, everything I say on the show is *vastly* exaggerated," Mom insisted. *Give it up, Mom*, my stern expression told her. Didn't matter. Tomato Lady wasn't listening to her anyhow.

"You remind me of my granddaughter," she prattled on. "She's just a bit clumsy and absentminded, too. I told her about your shoe flying off during a dance recital. The same thing happened to her!"

"Well, it's lovely to have met you," Mom said with the same clip in her voice she would use if a fire alarm sounded. She knew when I'd had enough and took no chances on my being snarky to kindly piano teachers.

Tomato Lady opened her mouth to respond, but Mom was already pushing the grocery cart past her. "Bye, now!"

Just for fun, I stayed planted in my spot for a couple of seconds. Mom grabbed my arm and I let out a vague yelp as I went flying behind her.

"Let's go!" she whispered when we were out of Tomato Lady's earshot.

"Oh, why, Mom?" I whined. "She hadn't even gotten to the part yet about the time I tried to hard-boil eggs in the microwave, or the time I scored a strike in the wrong bowling lane."

Mom couldn't help grinning. She tousled my hair with one hand as she pushed the cart with the other. "You're just so lovable," she cooed. "What can I say?"

"What *don't* you say?" I groused, but I smiled in spite of myself.

"I still haven't heard a word about camp," Mom said as we meandered down the aisle. "Tell me everything."

I shook my head. "My camp experience is not for public consignment."

Mom stifled a smile. "Consumption. Public consumption."

"Whatever. Hey! Don't use that on your show."

"Whole-wheat, Talia."

"What?"

"Get the whole-wheat bread, not the white."

"Are you even listening to me?" I grabbed a loaf of bread and tossed it in the cart.

"Yes, honey. Awful job. You hate it. I know." Mom put a check mark on her grocery list, then headed for the soup aisle as I trailed along.

"Why don't you get transferred to a different department?" I said. "Maybe you could *fix* TVs or something."

Mom pulled the grocery cart to a stop and turned to face me. "Honey, here's the thing," she said, putting her hands on my shoulders. "The stuff I talk about on the show is universal. People can relate because their kids do the same things. It's *kid* stuff. It's not *Talia* stuff."

"Wrong! Throwing up on my piano teacher was a Talia thing! None of her other students did it."

"But they *could* have," Mom said.

"But if they *did*, their moms wouldn't talk about it on TV. Mom, you've got to stop talking about me," I said, though she was already in motion again and putting check marks on her list. "I start middle school next week, and I think it's about time I start blending into the woodwork."

"French," Mom said.

"What?"

12

"French dressing, not ranch. We already have plenty of ranch at home."

I grabbed the bottle and tossed it into the cart as Mom made another check mark on her list.

"Honey, kids your age don't watch my show," she said absently, grabbing a bottle of catsup. "You have nothing to worry about."

"Then why did I get a get-well-soon card from my Girl Scout troop when you blabbed about my rash?"

Mom stopped again and squeezed my hand, smiling sweetly. "Honey, I know it isn't always easy having our life on display for the whole city. But it's my *job*. It's what I *do*. Tell ya what: if you'll stop doing funny things, I'll stop talking about them."

"Excellent point!" I said. "What's funny about throwing up on a piano teacher? That's an *un*funny thing. A sad thing. An intestinal-disorder kind of thing that most people would consider, oh, I don't know, *unfortunate*. So it doesn't matter what I do!"

"Talia," Mom said, "every job entails sacrifices. If I worked in a hospital, I'd have to leave you home alone during night shifts. If I drove a truck, I'd be on the road for days at a time. Doesn't my show seem like a pretty small sacrifice in the big scheme of things?"

By this point, I was trying to imagine my mother driving an eighteen-wheeler. And contemplating that being left alone for days at a time might just be the coolest thing in the world. "I wonder what the job market is like for truck drivers . . . ," I mused.

"Cheerios," my mom responded. "The big box."

3

"Mom!"

My screech practically shook the walls.

"Hi, honey," Mom said breezily as she walked in the door.

Mom knew this screech all too well. It was my *"How could you possibly embarrass me that way?"* screech when she got home from work. The one that began deep in the pit of my stomach, welled its way up my chest and spewed out of my throat like lava every time I saw her show.

Just look away, I'd tell myself when *Up and At 'Em* came on. *Pretend Mom's TV show is a documentary about protozoa. Just look away.*

But I never could. I'd have the remote control in my hand, ready to change the channel in an instant, but then I'd see a blip of Mom's show and know I was trapped. How could I look away? It would be like trying to ignore the jury when you're on trial for murder and they read your verdict. *Your Honor, we, the jury, find the defendant . . .* Just try blocking out the next word.

Anyhow, this show was particularly mortifying. Mom was talking to her cohost, Chad, about my starting sixth grade the following Monday. Here's a snippet:

CHAD: So Talia's finally back from camp, huh, Chels?

MOM: Finally. I missed her so much.

CHAD: Us, too, Chelsea. A whole week without any Talia stories? It was like going through withdrawal. You'll make up for lost time, I trust?

MOM: Oh, yeah. She starts middle school next week. It didn't really hit me until we picked up school supplies yesterday. Protractors! Can you believe that? Protractors are on her list.

CHAD: You have issues with protractors, do you?

MOM: As a matter of fact, I do. Considering that I'd completely forgotten what one looked like until Talia tossed it in the cart yesterday, I'm thinking she's outgrown the days when I could help her with her math homework. That's just wrong. It subverts the natural order for a kid to outpace her mother intellectually. It's like a baby chimp teaching her mom how to climb a tree.

CHAD: So multiplication tables are more your speed.

MOM: *Speed* being the definitive word, Chad. Why is Talia's childhood flying by so fast? Why am I filling my cart with protractors instead of crayons?

CHAD: Are you partial to any particular colors?

MOM: Talia always liked the scented ones. The only problem is she'd get a little overexuberant sniffing them. We actually ended up in the emergency room once to have them dug out of her nostrils. Blueberry Blast, as I recall.

CHAD: I'm guessing Talia won't be stuffing a protractor up her nose.

MOM: Hope not, Chad, but darned if I know what she will be doing with it. I don't know about Talia, but I'm just not ready for middle school.

"*Crayons up my nose?*"

"Now, honey . . ."

"The whole world needs to know I stuffed crayons up my nose?" I crumpled into a defeated heap on the sofa. "I'm ruined. *And one week before school starts!*"

"Talia, I told you, kids your age don't watch my show."

The phone rang, and without lifting my head from the sofa cushion, I reached to the end table, picked up the receiver and put it against my ear. "Hello?" I muttered miserably.

"Did you really shove crayons up your nose?" Bridget asked.

My scream was primal, the way cavemen screamed when they realized they couldn't outrun a mountain lion.

"Geez!" Bridget said. "Break my eardrum, why don't ya."

"Push me off a cliff, why don't ya," I responded.

Mom grabbed the phone from me. "Bridget, honey, it's really not a good time," she said. "Talia will call you later, okay? Okay."

She hung the phone up and smoothed my hair. "Honey, a lot of the stuff I talk about on the show, it's metaphorical, like when people tell you you're growing like a weed, which you are, incidentally."

"Well, I'm not a metaphor!" I snapped, jerking myself up to a sitting position. "I'm a real person who has to go to a real school and try to make friends with real kids who are imagining what color the inside of my nostrils is!"

Mom laughed into her hand.

"*It's not funny!*"

"Don't be mad," she pleaded. "Every parent can relate

to what I said. Don't you get it, honey? What I said was about you, but it wasn't really about you. It was about Everykid."

"Well, send Everykid to school next Monday, because I'm not going."

"Sure you are."

"No, I'm not, Mother," I said. "You have sealed my fate. I'm never going to school again. And because of you, I won't even be able to get a job in a crayon factory. So maybe your dream of keeping me a baby forever is coming true. I'm never getting off this couch. I hope you kept the receipt for the protractor."

Mom did a fake pout. "I'll get referred to social services if I don't send you to school," she said.

"Maybe you should get referred to social services for letting your kid shove crayons up her nose."

"No, they give you a pass on that one."

I buried my face under a pillow. "The whole world knows I'm a geek," I moaned.

"Honey, 'the whole world' is definitely an overstatement. True, the show is number one in its time slot, but the average viewer age is thirty-six-point-two, and . . ."

I buried my face deeper in the pillow. "You're a real laugh riot, Mom," I muttered. "Just tell me why I have to be the butt of the jokes."

Mom's eyes softened. She pulled the pillow away and put the palm of her hand against my cheek. "I'm sorry," she said in barely a whisper. "I really am. I didn't mean to embarrass you."

I sighed. "I know." It was easy to get mad at my mom. It was hard to stay mad at her. "But if you insist on keeping your job, could you at least homeschool me?"

"Sorry, honey," Mom said with a shrug. "I don't know how to use a protractor."

4

"Wow. They look so old."

Bridget and I had just loaded the dishwasher with our spaghetti-stained plates and were now plopped on her bed, thumbing through her brother's Crossroads Middle School yearbook. I gazed intently at the faces.

"You'll notice that not a single sixth grader has crayons stuffed up her nose, so you definitely need to move past that, Talia."

I playfully swatted Bridget's honey-colored ponytail. "If you don't quit watching my mother's show, I'm going to tell everyone in school your middle name."

Bridget's jaw dropped. "You wouldn't!"

"Bridget Luna Scott! Bridget Luna Scott!"

Bridget slapped her hand over my mouth. "Never utter those words again."

I laughed at her mock-stern expression. "We could call you Lunatic. Hey, by the way, what was your mother thinking when she named you that?"

"Something about a full moon on the night I was born," Bridget responded, flipping to another page. "At least, that's the long answer. The short answer is that she's certifiable."

"I heard that!" her mother called from the hall, making us giggle.

"No offense, Mom," Bridget called out cheerfully. "All mothers are certifiable."

"At least yours doesn't have her own TV show," I muttered. I pulled a lock of light brown hair behind my ear. "No way will I survive middle school if my mom keeps reminding the world what a loser I am."

Bridget turned to the clubs and activities section of the yearbook. "Speaking of TV shows"—she tapped a fingernail against the page she'd opened—"here's our ticket to fabulosity."

My eyebrows knitted together as I looked closer. "The Oddcast staff? No thanks."

The Crossroads Oddcast was a five-minute show of school announcements broadcast live on closed-circuit TV during homeroom each morning. The staff was small—about six to eight kids—and the staff rotated every three months: sixth graders the first three months, seventh graders the next three and eighth graders the last. The broadcasts could now be downloaded on computers as podcasts, so the name, the Crossroads Broadcast, had recently morphed into the Crossroads Oddcast.

"What's the big deal about making a few announcements

on TV?" I asked. "And who in their right mind would want to do a TV show in the first place?"

Bridget raised her hand. "I plan to be the sixth-grade director," she said in her done-deal tone of voice, "and you'll be one of the Oddcasters."

"Or not," I said, closing the book, but Bridget *tsked* and hastily reopened it to the same page.

"Isn't one celebrity in the family enough?" I asked.

"Now you're catching on," Bridget said, raising an eyebrow. "Your *mom*. Her experience will give us such an incredible edge. We'll be the most awesome Oddcast staff ever."

I gazed at her quizzically. "What do you care about directing, anyhow? I thought you wanted to be a lawyer."

"I'm keeping my options open."

"I'm opting out," I said, rising from the bed and mugging playfully in front of Bridget's mirror.

"See? You're a ham at heart," Bridget said. "Besides, what'll we do if we don't join the Oddcast?"

"There's always the pep squad," I said, piling my hair on top of my head and grinning exuberantly at my reflection. "Pom-poms are my favorite accessory, and I'm really good at mindless shrieking. Or I could join the math team. I *do* know my integers."

"Think about it, Talia," Bridget said, getting up from the bed and talking to my reflection in the mirror. "It drives you crazy when your mom talks about you on TV, right?"

"Yeah?" I said.

"Well, if you were an Oddcaster, the shoe would be on the other foot. *You'd* be the one with a microphone."

She had that silly, satisfied grin on her face, the one I

pictured her having in the courtroom twenty years from now when she was outsmarting somebody on the witness stand.

"Don't Oddcasters just give school announcements?" I asked. "You know, ice cream's on sale in the cafeteria? Don't forget to wear your school ID? That kinda thing? I can't exactly picture my mother freaking out about that."

"You're thinking too small, Talia," Bridget said. "The Oddcast doesn't have to be only school announcements just because that's the way it's always been done before. My brother was on the staff last year, and he said if I come to the auditions with a lot of great ideas, there's a good chance I'll be named the director. And with a new director at the helm"—she tapped her chest—"things could be very different this year. You could do your own little commentary. We'll call it 'Talia Talk.' "

My eyebrows knitted together.

"Not a bad idea," I murmured. "If my mom gets to tell the whole world what a nutcase I am, why shouldn't I have a chance to undo the damage?"

"Now you're talking, girlfriend."

"Still," I said, "what makes you think we'll get permission to do a commentary?"

Bridget put her hands on her hips. "Leave that," she said, "to the director."

5

Cough.

Chalky-white powder filled my nostrils as Grandma sprinkled flour on her hands.

"Grab me that rolling pin, will you, honey?" she said. I waved away the flour cloud, handed her the rolling pin and watched as she pressed it against the cookie dough she'd plopped on the counter. She hummed as she rolled, the corners of her mouth pressed into a little smile.

"You're always in a good mood," I told her, smiling back.

She glanced at me with twinkly brown eyes. "I'm in a good mood anytime you're around, and that's the only time you ever see me," she teased.

"She's right," said Grandpa, picking up an apple and taking a bite as he walked into the kitchen. "When you're not around, she growls like a bear."

Grandma growled at him, and we all laughed.

I studied Grandma's face as she pressed the dough.

"Did Dad look like you?" I asked casually.

She looked up, startled. "You remember what your father looked like, Talia," she said, but I wasn't sure if it was a question or a statement. "And heaven knows we have plenty of pictures around."

"He looked like me, the handsome devil," Grandpa said, making me shriek in surprise when he kissed the back of my neck.

"He looked like your grandpa when he was a baby," Grandma said. "Both bald."

Grandpa growled at her and took another bite of his apple.

"I wonder if Dad would have turned bald if he'd lived long enough," I said, then wished I could snatch back the words. My grandparents sucked in their breath and looked at each other for just a second before Grandma's eyes turned misty. She stared down at her dough and pursed her lips.

"Sorry, Grandma," I mumbled. It always caught me off guard when she turned sad thinking about my dad. Most of the time these days, talking about him only made her laugh, and I loved to see her laugh. But sometimes, like the time we planted pansies and she remembered doing the same thing with him years earlier, her face would crinkle like an autumn leaf, and out would come the tears.

Grandma swallowed hard. "Don't be silly, sweetie," she said in a fake-cheery voice. "You can always ask me anything about your dad."

Grandpa put an arm around each of our waists. "Why

are we talking about baldies?" he asked, giving a little squeeze. "I'd much rather talk about you, missy. Are you excited about your first day of school tomorrow?"

"I'm thinking about joining the Crossroads Oddcast," I said as Grandma and I began pressing star-shaped cookie cutters into the dough.

"What in the world is that?" Grandma asked.

"It's a broadcast and a podcast. A podcast is like . . . it's like watching TV on your computer."

"My," Grandma said, which was what she said anytime the subject of computers came up.

"It's basically just a few students giving announcements on TV during homeroom each morning," I continued. "The sixth graders do it the first part of the year, then the seventh graders, then the eighth graders. I thought maybe I'd audition for the sixth-grade staff."

"Oh!" Grandma said, her face brightening. "Just like your mom."

"Kinda," I said, pressing the cookie cutter into another section of dough. "Bridget wants to be the director."

Grandma and Grandpa exchanged glances. They'd known Bridget a long time.

"What about Meredith and Brynne?" Grandma asked. "Are they going to audition, too?"

I shrugged. No use going into the whole "that's so over" explanation about our friendship. Grandma would look all devastated and talk about what lovely girls they were.

Grandpa walked by and snipped off a piece of cookie dough, popping it into his mouth.

Grandma slapped his hand playfully. "Howard, please!

Just finish your apple and leave our cookies alone, at least until they're baked."

"Raw cookie dough can make you sick," I told him earnestly. "Uncooked eggs. Salmonella. We learned about it in health class."

He coughed and sputtered. "Thanks. You really know how to whet a fella's appetite. Is that the kind of wisdom you're going to dispense on your modcast?"

"Oddcast," I corrected him, giggling. "And I don't even know if I'll make the staff."

"You can do anything you set your mind to," Grandma said, nodding smartly and putting a cookie sheet in the oven.

I spontaneously kissed her on the cheek. If only she knew I'd be lucky to make the B list at school, maybe even the C list since Mom's crayon announcement, she wouldn't be nearly so confident. Or on the other hand, maybe she would. That was the thing about grandmothers.

"*Pssssst.*"

I turned around in my desk. "What?" I whispered to Bridget.

Bridget cupped her hand around her mouth. "I think Meredith must have gotten some awful disease at camp." She tossed her head in Meredith's direction, and I looked two rows over. "It's like the veins around her eyes are about to pop out of her head."

I giggled. "That's blue eye shadow," I said.

As soon as Bridget and I had settled into our homeroom for the first day of school, our eyes were wandering up and down the rows, checking people out. Lots of the faces were unfamiliar . . . kids from different elementary schools who somehow seemed much more pulled together than I felt. Of the ones I knew, some hadn't changed much over the summer. Bobbi Kay Banks still had crooked bangs. Aubrey Merrill still wore a matching hair bow, blouse and shoelaces. Savannah Callahan still wore T-shirts with pictures of kittens. Trey Hayes still had wadded-up tissues in his pants pocket. (Allergies.)

But some people had definitely changed. Meredith and Brynne looked even more high-maintenance than they had at camp. Blue eye shadow was only one of the new colors on Mer's face. Pink circles glowed on her cheeks. Her lips were gooey with the same cotton-candy shade. Her wavy hair was suddenly sleek and straight. She looked annoyed when she caught my eye and quickly looked away.

Meredith whispered something to Brynne, who glanced at me and looked annoyed, too. Brynne's shirt was snug and her earrings dangly. Her hair looked like it smelled good. And the way she tossed it off her shoulder—did she practice that sort of thing in front of the mirror?

"Those two look like they wiped their hands on their faces after finger painting," Bridget said. Meredith and Brynne exchanged whispers with cupped hands, then shot us icy glares. Bridget gave them a fake smile and waved heartily, adding the "call me" gesture as a finishing touch.

"Bridget!" I scolded, sinking lower into my seat.

Ms. Perkins stood up from her desk at the front of the classroom. "Okay, class, time to settle down," she said. "I'll call the roll in a minute, but first, I want to go over a few things and I need your full attention, so let's get serious."

Bridget made her goofy cheeks-sucked-in-like-a-piranha expression and we dissolved into laughter.

"Girls!"

We bit our lips in response to Ms. Perkins's booming voice.

"Very mature," Meredith said with a sneer.

"Actually, maturity is one of the very subjects I was just about to discuss," Ms. Perkins said, which would have been the perfect time for Bridget and me to share another goofy look—maybe our concerned-index-finger-on-the-chin expression—but we both thought better of it. "You're in middle school now, meaning it's time to start acting like young adults. Up until this year, you've been taking baby steps. First grade to second grade? Baby step. Second grade to third grade? Baby step. Third grade to fourth grade? Baby step. Fourth grade to fifth grade?"

"Step on it, will ya, Ms. Perkins?" Bridget whispered behind me.

"Baby step," Ms. Perkins continued. "Fifth grade to sixth grade?" She paused for effect, then raised a single eyebrow. "Giant step."

"I guess that explains Trey Ackerman's size-twelve sneakers," Bridget whispered.

"You're not boys and girls anymore," Ms. Perkins said solemnly, walking back and forth with her hands folded in front of her. "You're young ladies and gentlemen. It's time to 'step up' the maturity, if you will."

I could practically feel Bridget about to jump out of her skin from the effort of holding in her snappy response.

"Can anyone tell me what might differentiate a mature middle school student from an immature elementary school student?" Ms. Perkins asked.

Brynne raised her hand primly.

"Yes?" Ms. Perkins asked.

"A mature student doesn't make silly faces," Brynne replied, casting a disapproving glance at Bridget.

Bridget crossed her eyes and stuck her tongue out the side of her mouth for a split second, but rebounded to a sweet smile by the time Ms. Perkins's eyes settled on her.

"Okay," Ms. Perkins said slowly. "Anyone else? Another example of what differentiates a mature student from an immature student?"

Meredith raised her hand, then cleared her throat when Ms. Perkins called on her. "A mature student knows that acting like a baby will get you nowhere in life."

Bridget's eyebrows shot up in mock horror as Meredith cast her eyes pointedly in her direction. "*Me?*" Bridget mouthed, pointing at her chest.

"*Yes, you,*" Meredith mouthed back.

Now it was Bridget's turn to raise her hand, and she didn't bother waiting to be called on. "Ms. Perkins, I think a sign of maturity is the ability to listen to constructive criticism without pointing out that the constructive criticizers' blush isn't blended very well into their cheeks. Is that a word? Criticizers?"

Meredith and Brynne dropped their jaws. Ms. Perkins put her hands on her hips and stomped one foot as the class twittered.

I sighed and glanced at my watch. It had taken Bridget a grand total of five minutes to start us on the road to middle school dweebdom.

• • •

I made a beeline for Bridget as soon as I saw her in the cafeteria. We'd had separate classes and hadn't seen each other since homeroom, so lunchtime was our first chance to hang out.

I got right to the point. "Are you insane?"

Bridget crinkled her nose. "Chicken strips or salad bar? I can't decide."

"Bridget! Focus! Making fun of Meredith and Brynne on the first day of school? That's crazy even for you!"

Bridget headed toward the salad bar. I grabbed my cafeteria tray and followed.

"It feels like such a giant step, having to choose what to eat for lunch rather than having a hairnet lady plop something on my plate," Bridget said. "Am I really mature enough to make my own lunch choice?" She clutched her heart for full dramatic effect. "Am I ready for . . . *the salad bar?*"

She grabbed some tongs and dropped lettuce onto her plate.

"Bridget!" I said. "I know they were acting snotty, but we *are* all friends, you know—or we *were*, anyway—and it's not like we have popularity to spare as it is, and did you notice the look you got from Ms. Perkins? You were like one baby step away from detention. How would you explain detention on the first day of school? Your mother would kill you."

She picked through the cherry tomatoes, putting the mushy pale ones back and placing the firm red ones on her plate. "Talia, murder would definitely be an overreaction to detention. I'm thinking anger-management classes would be in order."

I groaned. "You cannot go through middle school this way," I said through gritted teeth. "You're my BFF, and I have a reputation to consider."

She stopped poking through the tomatoes long enough to look me squarely in the eye. "Talia, your reputation is for stuffing crayons up your nose."

"And that being the case, it helps me that you tick off Meredith and Brynne on the first day of school?"

Bridget sprinkled grated cheese on her salad. "Since when do you care what Meredith and Brynne think?"

"Since I would prefer not to be labeled Dweeb of the Universe on the first day of school!"

I huffed in exasperation. The most lovable things about Bridget were also the most infuriating. Yes, it was fun to have a total goofball for a best friend . . . *sometimes*. Yes, I loved clutching my sides with laughter . . . *on occasion*. Yes, off-the-charts zaniness was refreshing . . . *in small doses*.

"Somebody needs a chill pill," Bridget said in a singsong voice. Then her eyes locked on someone across the room. "Talia, that's Ms. Stephens," she said.

"Our language arts teacher?"

"Yeah. I recognize her from the yearbook."

"So what?"

"She's the Oddcast advisor, remember?"

"Oh . . ."

Bridget walked to a table with her salad, put it down and cupped her hands around her mouth. "Ms. Stephens!" she called. "Yo, Ms. Stephens!"

"*Bridget!*" I moaned, putting my empty tray beside her salad and burying my face in my hands.

"What? I thought you wanted to audition."

"I *do*, but . . ." I turned with a jerk as I realized Ms. Stephens had walked up to our table. She had strawberry-blond hair and pretty blue eyes.

"No shouting across the cafeteria, please," she told us, but her tone was friendly.

"Sorry," Bridget said. "But here's the thing: we want to audition for the Oddcast." She pointed from me back to herself. "She's Talia Farrow. I'm Bridget Scott. We're in your language arts class. Talia's mom has her own show, so Talia kinda has TV stardom in her genes. You're still the advisor, right?"

Ms. Stephens nodded. "Who's your mom?" she asked me.

I blushed. "Chelsea Farrow."

Her face brightened. "*Up and At 'Em!* I love that show. I always watch it when I'm not at work. Your mom does a great job."

"Which is why we would be such a good addition to the Oddcast staff," Bridget said. "Her mom could teach us everything she knows. I'm thinking I could be the director. And as the director—assuming you made me the director, of course—I'd like to make a few changes to the Oddcast, kinda spice it up."

Ms. Stephens sucked in her cheeks. "Is that right?"

"Oh, I have a ton of ideas," Bridget said, warming to the subject. "My brother was on the eighth-grade Oddcast staff last year—Brad Scott?—and according to him, the Oddcast is so dull, it doubles as a snooze alarm: Oddcast's on, time to catch a few z's. Oddcast's over—time to wake up and start first period. Ya know?"

Ms. Stephens's eyes narrowed.

"No offense," Bridget assured her. "You work with what you've got, right? You get a bunch of boring kids with monotone voices and the creative instincts of a gnat, and, well, you do the best you can with what you have to work with. But I think this is the year we could make the Oddcast the best it's ever been."

Ms. Stephens's expression softened a bit as Bridget came up for air. "You're certainly enthusiastic," she said evenly.

"Oh, we really are," Bridget gushed as I stared at my shoes. "And we're hard workers, too. We'd do a great job for you, Ms. Stephens, really we would, and I was thinking Talia could—"

"Does Talia speak? That's kind of a prerequisite for an Oddcaster," Ms. Stephens said.

My cheeks got hot.

"Oh, she talks," Bridget said. "And she's funny, like her mom. That's why I was thinking we'd give her a chatty spot on the Oddcast. We could call it 'Talia Talk.' "

Ms. Stephens tapped her fingers together. "You've thought this through," she told Bridget.

"Oh, definitely. A director always has to be one step ahead, you know."

Ms. Stephens's eyes locked with mine. "A commentary's not a bad idea. But commentaries have to be written. Do you like to write?"

"Loves to," Bridget answered. I dug my fingernails into my palms.

"Why don't you show me a sample of your writing before the Oddcast auditions next week?" Ms. Stephens said.

"Unnecessary," Bridget responded. "Her writing is brilliant. Trust me."

I shot daggers at Bridget through narrowed eyes, but she didn't notice. Ms. Stephens looked at her in that amusement-turning-into-irritation expression that Bridget had a knack for bringing out in people.

"Yes, I can bring you a sample of my writing," I told Ms. Stephens, nervously smoothing my green T-shirt.

Ms. Stephens put her hands in her slacks pockets. "What kinds of things would you write about?" she asked me.

My stomach lurched to my throat. Bridget might have thought this through, but *I* hadn't. Bridget opened her mouth to speak, but Ms. Stephens, still looking straight at me, held up her hand to stop her.

I cleared my throat. "Just whatever's going on in my life, I guess," I said. "How to get through PE class when you're really awful at sports, or how to pull something from the bottom of your locker without all your books crashing down on your head—stuff like that."

Ms. Stephens winked at me. "Suppose you have your writing sample to me by next Monday," she said.

"Oh, she'll have it for you tomorrow," Bridget volunteered.

Ms. Stephens nodded sharply. "Tomorrow it is. But no guarantees." Her eyes darted to Bridget. "That goes for you, too."

Bridget saluted her. Ms. Stephens smiled. "See you girls next period."

She walked back to her table as I stared down at my empty tray. "Bridget!" I moaned. "Here's the deal with having you for a friend: suddenly I have extra homework, *and* I have no lunch."

"You can thank me for the homework, but you'll have to fix your own lunch tray."

I stomped my foot, just missing her toe.

She grinned, stepping back. "You expect me to do everything for you?"

7

I kissed Grandma on the cheek when I got home from school, wolfed down a snack in the kitchen, then headed to my bedroom to do my homework. (Yes! Homework on the first day!) I breezed through math and English, struggled through science, read my social studies chapter, then moved on to the fun part. I walked from my desk to my bed, fluffed the pillows, snuggled against them and started typing on my laptop:

SAMPLE COMMENTARY FOR THE CROSSROADS ODDCAST

Talia Talk

It's official: I'm in middle school now. I've just gotten started, but here are a few things

I've learned so far that might help my fellow newbies:

• Locker combinations are trickier than they look.

• Kicking your locker doesn't make it any easier to open.

• Tricky locker combinations can make you late for class, and you get detention even if you're limping to class with a broken toe.

• Middle school teachers don't remind you to do your homework. They just give you a zero if you don't have it. I think the teachers get off pretty easy with this low-maintenance approach, but there you have it.

• Since I'll be in middle school the next three years, learn how to pronounce my name. I get "Ta-LEE-ah" a lot, as in "See ya, Ta-LEE-ah, wouldn't want to be ya." Here's an i-DEE-ya: learn how to pronounce TAL-ia, shall ya?

• Friend amnesia starts in middle school. Kids who've known each other since kindergarten start sixth grade and it's like the hard drives in their brains crash. Bam! Suddenly you're perfect strangers. Time to reboot your friendship hard drive. Weird but true.

I'm sure I have lots more to learn, but that's all my brain can handle for now. Best of luck, fellow newbies. Signing off for now, this is Talia Farrow for the Crossroads Oddcast.

"Talia?" *Tap, tap.*

I jumped with a start and hit Save.

"Talia?" my mother called again from behind my closed bedroom door.

"Yes, Mom?"

She opened the door and walked in. "How was your first day of school?" she asked with a wide smile, bouncing on the balls of her feet.

I glanced at my watch. "It's after five already?" Grandma stayed with me in the afternoons until Mom got home from work. I must not have heard Grandma calling goodbye as my mom walked in. I'd lost track of time typing away.

"Yup," Mom said. "I just got home. So how was school?"

"Okay." I glanced self-consciously at the laptop. Was my writing any good, or was it hopelessly lame? If I made the Oddcast staff, I'd find out soon enough.

"Did you like your teachers? Your classes? Tell me everything."

I shrugged as Mom sat down on the bed beside me. "Bridget totally humiliated me," I said.

Mom gasped. "On the first day? What did she do?"

"She was just . . . herself," I said, and Mom nodded knowingly.

She laced her fingers in her lap. "What happened?"

I sat up straighter and hugged my knees against my chest. "She's just kinda . . . loud, you know? I don't want everybody in school thinking I'm a dweeb. Meredith and Brynne were treating us like we had blood oozing from our eyeballs or something."

Mom winced. "Thanks for the visual." She squeezed my

hand. "It's just the first day, honey. I'm sure you'll all be hanging out together soon, just like always."

I bit my bottom lip. "I don't know, Mom. Things seem different now. I'm thinking I can have Bridget for a friend, or I can have Meredith and Brynne for friends, but I can't have both." I sucked in my breath. "But of *course* Bridget will always be my best friend. I'd rather not have *any* friends than to lose Bridget as a friend." Why was I talking so fast? "And I'm starting to think that Brynne and Meredith are total snobs anyway. Who wants snobs for friends? Bridget's a true friend. So what if she's a little loud?"

I nodded sharply. Problem solved. But Mom looked a bit concerned.

"Honey, you don't have to work everything out on the first day. Give things time to sort themselves out. Every friend has flaws, but you're right: true friends stand the test of time."

I wrinkled my nose. "Mom, you sound like a bumper sticker."

She tickled me and giggled, then said, "Well, you're having a bumper-sticker moment."

"I just wish I could shove a chill pill down Bridget's throat sometimes, you know?"

Mom raised an eyebrow. "I have an idea. How about burgers for dinner? We'll take Bridget, and I can drop a few hints about playing it cool in school, at least for the first few days while everyone's still testing the waters."

I drummed my fingers on my laptop. "Burgers sound great. But go easy on the advice. I don't want Bridget to think I'm turning into a narc or something."

Mom's jaw dropped. "Narc? Talia, do you even know what that means?"

I shrugged. "A fink? I heard someone say it in school today."

Mom shook her head and smiled. "Middle school has definitely arrived," she murmured, then patted my leg. "Call Bridget. I'm starving."

● ● ●

"So then Meredith says something really snotty, so then *I* say something like 'Criticizers should at least blend in their blush before they criticize other people,' making a mental note about whether *criticizer* is an actual word, so then Ms. Perkins says—"

"Bridget," I said calmly while eating my burger in our red vinyl booth, "come up for air."

Bridget swallowed. "She asked!" she said, nodding toward my mom.

Mom dipped a fry in catsup and popped it into her mouth. "You know, Bridget," she said, "sometimes when you're starting something new, like middle school, the best approach is to lie low for a while—you know, keep a low profile—and get the lay of the land before you start putting yourself out there."

Don't go there, Mom, I was thinking.

Bridget looked at her blankly. "Out where?"

Mom looked confused. "What?"

"Out where?" Bridget repeated. "You know, putting my-self out there. Where is there?"

Mom nibbled on a fry. "Well, using today as an example, 'there' is out on a limb, with Meredith and Brynne being mad at you and Ms. Perkins maybe getting the wrong impression about what a sweet girl you are. Maybe if you'd kept a lower profile—"

"Chelsea, is that you?"

We all looked up toward the sound of the voice and saw Meredith's mom walking toward us. Uh-oh . . . that probably meant . . .

"Hi, Peggy!" Mom said. "Hi, Meredith!"

Meredith, hovering behind her mom, curled her mouth into a half-smile.

"Loved your show Friday," Meredith's mom said. "Crayons up the nose! I remember those days!"

Meredith cleared her throat loudly and jerked her head toward another table.

"Thanks," Mom said. "Of course, the crayons-up-the-nose story was a bit of an exaggeration. You know, creative license."

Nice try, Mom.

"Oh, I know how mischievous Talia can be," Meredith's mom said, grinning at me. "Remember when she sneaked up behind the dancing bear at the pizza parlor during Meredith's birthday party and pulled the bottom of his costume down, almost taking the poor guy's pants off in the process? You've *got* to talk about that on your show!"

"*Mother!*" Meredith whispered, jerking her head toward the empty table again.

The two moms laughed lightly while I sank deeper into the booth. Mom glanced at me, then cleared her throat.

"Talia has outgrown that kind of behavior, of course," she said.

Meredith raised an eyebrow.

"Did you girls enjoy your first day of school?" Meredith's mom asked.

"Hit and miss," Bridget responded. "You know, at first blush, everything seemed to be going fine, and then . . ."

I glared at her.

"Well," Meredith's mom said quickly, "maybe tomorrow will go more smoothly. The first day is always a little rocky."

"Maybe Meredith can move to the desk by mine," Bridget said cheerfully. "She sets such a good example."

"Mother!" Meredith spat. "Our food is getting cold!"

"What food? We haven't ordered yet," her mom replied, but Meredith grabbed her by the arm and started pulling her away. The moms murmured their goodbyes, and Bridget waved heartily, making the "call me" sign to Meredith.

Mom and I exchanged glances. "Um, Bridget . . . ," Mom said.

"I know, Mrs. Farrow. Low profile. I kinda speak before I think sometimes. Bad habit. Definitely something I need to work on."

Mom sighed and bit into her hamburger. Bridget could leave anybody speechless.

"So did Talia tell you the news?" Bridget said, bouncing in her seat.

Mom looked clueless.

"We're auditioning for the Crossroads Oddcast," Bridget said through a mouthful of fries. "I want to be the director."

"Is that so," Mom said dryly.

"I'm really gonna spice things up. Up until now, the show has been nothing but boring school announcements: 'The library's closed tomorrow.' 'Interim reports go out next week.' Blah, blah, blah."

"And you have a better idea?" Mom asked.

"A zillion of them. Like, instead of the Oddcasters sitting behind a desk talking into the camera, we could do live remotes from the cafeteria or the gym. We could have kids rap the weather instead of just telling it. And—here's where Talia comes in—we're adding a commentary so Talia can tell funny little stories like you do."

Mom's eyebrows knitted together. "You've really thought this through."

"That's what Ms. Stephens said," Bridget said proudly. "She's the Oddcast advisor."

"Bridge, there's that little matter of auditions," I reminded her patiently.

"Right. But with your help, Mrs. Farrow, we're in."

Mom smiled. "I'd love to help!" she said. "Just think, Talia . . . now you'll be the one with the microphone."

I took a sip of my soft drink. "Don't get too excited, Mom," I said, grinning at her. "Payback can be brutal."

8

"Hmmmmm."

That's all she'd said so far.

"Hmmmmm." Louder this time.

Ms. Stephens had asked me to stop by her class after lunch the next day so she could look at the Oddcast essay I'd drafted. She adjusted her glasses a couple of times as she read it. I think I saw a tiny smile at one point, but that might have just been the way her lips curved when she said, "Hmmmmm."

Finally, she put the essay on her desk, took her glasses off and held them in her hand.

"Nice," she told me.

"I didn't have much time to work on it," I said, staring at my hands as I rubbed them together.

"You have a nice style." There was that word again. "Lots of energy, but a light touch."

I managed a weak smile.

"But I have to warn you, Talia: we've never tried a commentary on the Oddcast before, and writing one regularly isn't as easy as you might think. It can be hard to come up with different topics."

"I really like to write," I said simply.

Ms. Stephens nodded. "Once a week might be doable." She leaned forward and smiled. "Auditions are Monday after school. Be there. I think you'll make a terrific addition to our staff."

● ● ●

Bridget was waiting for me when I walked out of Ms. Stephens's room.

"So? Did she like your essay?"

I tossed a lock of hair over my shoulder. "She thought it was okay," I said. But who was I kidding? I couldn't play it cool with Bridget. I broke into a grin and said, "She said she thinks I'll make a great addition to the staff!"

Bridget squealed, grabbed my arms and broke into a dance.

"Bridget!" I yelped as she twirled me around.

"This is huge!" Bridget said. "We'll make such a great team. I've already written a list of ideas for the show to help me nail the director spot."

A teacher walked past us and scowled.

"Bridget, we'll be late for class," I whispered, untangling our arms.

Kids started filing into Ms. Stephens's room for her next class, knocking our shoulders lightly to squeeze through the doorway.

"A little respect, please!" Bridget told them way too loudly. "This is the Oddcast commentator you're shoving. Hey, the fingers! Watch the fingers! She's gotta write with those!"

Uh-oh. Here came Meredith and Brynne. Meredith jutted out her chin. "You are so loud," she told Bridget. Brynne nodded.

"Loud, proud and unbowed," Bridget retorted, then took a bow.

"Who even talks like that?" Meredith asked Brynne, rolling her eyes and squeezing past us to get through Ms. Stephens's door.

"Freaks talk like that," Brynne murmured.

My heart sank. "I've got to get to my seat before the bell rings," I told Bridget.

"Just don't use up all your brain cells in class," she said. "We've got auditions to prepare for. Remember, we're a team."

That was what worried me.

Tap, tap, tap.

I closed my science book, laid it on my desk and glanced toward my bedroom door. "Yes?"

"Just me," Mom said, opening the door.

"Hi, Mom."

I heard my grandma call goodbye from the living room as she headed home for the evening.

Mom walked over to my desk. "So how was school today?"

"Pretty good. I wrote a sample essay for the Oddcast, and Ms. Stephens liked it."

Mom smiled. "That's terrific, honey. You've always been such a great writer."

"Writing's just the first part," I said. "If I make the Oddcast staff, I'll have to actually read what I've written—

on live TV. Can you help Bridge and me practice over the weekend? Auditions are Monday."

"Oooh, I'd love to. See? I told you my job wasn't so bad."

I wrinkled my nose.

"How did it go with Bridget today?" Mom asked.

I sighed. "Same as usual. That little speech you gave her last night about keeping a low profile? Dream on."

"So she didn't take it down a notch?"

"She can be so embarrassing, Mom," I said through clenched teeth. "True, Meredith and Brynne have turned into total snobs, but they'd probably be nice enough if Bridget didn't make us seem like freaks."

Mom frowned. "How can *Bridget* make *you* seem like a freak?"

"Guilt by assassination."

Mom held her hand over her mouth, but I could still see her smile. "Association," she said. "Guilt by association."

"Whatever. Hey! Don't use that on your show."

Mom zipped her lip. "Scout's honor. So, ya hungry?"

"Kinda."

"How about if we go out for pizza?" Mom said, shifting her weight and shoving her hands into her pockets.

I peered at her quizzically. "Burgers last night and pizza tonight? I hope the nutrition police don't find out."

"Well, if you don't *want* pizza . . ."

"No, no. Pizza works."

"Good." Mom paused, cleared her throat and stood straighter. "Mind if a friend comes along?"

"No thanks! I need a break from Bridget."

Mom chewed her bottom lip. "Actually, I meant a friend of *mine*."

"Which friend? Joanne?"

Mom shook her head.

"Claire?"

"Nope."

Why wouldn't Mom look at me? "I'm running out of your friends," I said, looking at her suspiciously.

Mom finally looked me in the eye. "His name is Jake."

His name? "A guy friend?"

"A guy who's a friend," she said quickly. "He works at the station."

"Jake," I repeated, more to myself than to Mom. "Sounds like somebody on a soap opera. Somebody with a mysterious past."

"It's just a name. And he's just a friend."

I leaned closer toward Mom, squinting. "Mom? Are you blushing?"

Mom waved her hand in front of her face. "Oh, for heaven's sake!"

"You are! You're blushing!" I gasped. "Wait a minute. Are we going on a *date* tonight?"

"Oh, Talia!"

I couldn't help giggling. I wasn't used to seeing Mom nervous and fidgety. But then, I'd never thought of my mom dating, either. In the four years since Dad had died, she'd never seemed the slightest bit interested in any other man. Her friends tried to fix her up every once in a while—even Grandma and Grandpa introduced her to a couple of people from their church choir—but Mom always blew them off, saying she had a daughter to raise, a job to do, a house to clean and no time for or interest in a love life.

"Is he cute?" I asked Mom, bouncing in my chair.

"Talia Farrow, you stop it this instant! This is not a date! This is pizza with a friend." She nodded sharply. "Pizza. With a friend."

The doorbell rang and my eyes widened. "Jake? Jake, mah dahlin', is that you?" I said in a Scarlett O'Hara accent, clutching my heart and swooning.

"Talia!" Mom whispered, looking stern and panicky at the same time. "Please don't embarrass me!"

"My smellin' salts! Hand me my smellin' salts, won't you, dahlin'? The thought of seein' Jake makes me feel downright faint." I swooned right out of my chair and plopped onto the floor.

"You. Will. Behave," Mom whispered firmly. "Or no extra pizza toppings."

I laughed as I picked myself up off the floor and watched Mom walk down the hall toward the front door. I heard the door squeak open. Next came the rumbling sound of a low voice, then Mom's voice sounding like clinking crystal. This really *was* weird.

After a few minutes, Mom called, "Talia, honey? Can you come here? There's someone I'd like you to meet."

I tightened my ponytail and walked down the hall into the living room. A tall, skinny guy with a dark beard and mustache smiled at me and held out his hand.

"Jake, this is my daughter, Talia," Mom said as he shook my hand. "Talia, this is Jake."

"Talia Farrow," Jake said, his brown eyes twinkling. "Your mom must be a fan of Booker T. Washington."

I shrugged, confused.

"The *T* in his name stands for Taliaferro," he said. "Talia Farrow . . . Taliaferro . . ." His voice trailed off.

"Right," I said evenly.

"I didn't think about that until after she was born and a couple of people pointed it out," Mom said. "So he wasn't technically her namesake—not that I wouldn't be proud to have her named after such a prestigious man. I mean, he was remarkable, such an outstanding contributor to civil rights and higher education. . . ." Mom's voice trailed off. She cleared her throat and twirled a piece of hair.

"Is your first name Booker?" Jake asked, then laughed, which caused Mom to laugh too loudly.

Jake clapped his hands in a single, loud *thwack* that made me jump.

"So," he said, "is anybody ready for pizza?"

Mom raised her hand. "Me," she said, shooting me a glance that made me figure I was supposed to raise my hand too, so I did, kinda, then realized I looked ridiculous and put it back down. This day was just getting too bizarre.

Jake opened the front door and flung out his arm. "After you, ladies."

Mom and I walked out the door. Jake followed, accidentally slamming the front door way too hard.

"Oops! My bad," he said as we walked toward his car. "That's the expression these days, Talia, right?"

"What?" I asked, but Mom gave me another desperate-looking glance that made me say, "Oh. Right."

Jake opened the back door of his car and hastily moved some papers from the seat to clear a spot for me. "Sorry," he said. "I'm not used to backseat passengers."

I wasn't used to *being* a backseat passenger.

I coughed as I settled into his dusty little car, fastened my seat belt and studied the back of Jake's head as he sat in the driver's seat. *What do we really know about this guy?* I found myself wondering. *Mom wouldn't put me in the backseat of just anybody's car, would she? Certainly she knows him pretty well . . . right? Maybe not. Regardless, what do I really know about Mom's taste in guys? He could be a serial killer, for all we know. . . .*

"So tell me about yourself, Talia," Jake said.

"Oh, there's not much to tell. What about you?"

"Talia!" Mom scolded, but Jake laughed.

"It's okay," he said. "Me. Hmmm. Okay, here goes: My name is Jake Reynolds, I'm a sportscaster for WBJM—"

"Right. I thought you looked familiar."

"Yet thinner and taller in person, right? Okay, so I'm a sportscaster, I like surfing and playing the guitar—usually not at the same time—um, I like to read, I have a dog named E-bay—"

"E-bay?" I said.

"Yeah, but I didn't name him after the Web site; I had another dog named Freeway and I thought E-bay sounded like a good name for Freeway's brother, not that they were technically related, of course, and Freeway has since died, but of old age and not in a car-related accident, as you might suspect, so now it's just me and E-bay—sorry, I mean E-bay and *me*—" He shot a playful glance at Mom.

"And coincidentally, E-bay barks whenever I log on to my eBay account, so he probably thinks he's the CEO or something. . . ."

I couldn't help but laugh. Mom tossed me a grateful smile from the front seat.

"So how did you and Mom meet?" I asked.

"We were hiking in the Himalayas," Jake said, and it took me a second to realize he was teasing. He winked at me through the rearview mirror. "Actually, we hang out in the same studio for eight or nine hours a day, so there was a certain inevitability. Still, it took me eight months to wear her down."

I bit my lower lip. "So this *is* a date," I said, not sure whether it was a statement or a question.

"It's pizza with a friend," Mom said quickly.

"In my case, pizza with *two* friends," Jake said. "But I like the sound of *date*. It has definite potential. Put in a good word for me, will you, Talia? I'm a nice guy."

"Says who?" I asked with a smile.

"Well, E-bay would say it, if he could talk," Jake replied. "But his drool speaks volumes. Oh, and my mom says nice things about me too. Would you like her number?"

"Moms *have* to say nice things about their kids," I reasoned.

"So it's objective character references you're looking for," Jake said, rubbing his beard with one hand while he steered with the other. "Tell ya what: I'll dust off my resume and give you a copy next time I take your mom out on a . . . er, next time we go out for pizza."

Next time, huh? This really *was* a date . . . which should

have been fine, right? Especially with a guy who named his dog E-bay and didn't mind an eleven-year-old kid hanging around. *Yes*, I told myself sharply. *It's okay.*

But why was my stomach suddenly hurting?

● ● ●

My hair was still damp from the shower as I brushed it in front of my bedroom mirror.

Mom walked down the hall, then hovered in my doorway.

"How ya doin'?" she asked, fingering a button on her pajama top.

"Fine," I responded, still staring into the mirror. I tilted my chin upward. "You could've given me a little notice, you know."

Mom's slippers scuffed along my hardwood floor as she walked toward me. She ran her fingers through my damp hair. "I didn't want it to seem like a big deal," she said softly. "And it wasn't. It was just pizza. Jake asked me right before I left the studio, and I thought, *Why not?* It's not like we planned it six months in advance."

I peered at her reflection in the mirror. "*Eight* months," I corrected her. "That's how long he said he's been trying to get you to go out with him."

Mom sighed. "Honey, I haven't been even remotely interested in dating since your dad died. And maybe I'm still not. But Jake is good company and . . . this felt right. But it *wasn't* a big deal."

I ran the brush through my hair, brushing away Mom's fingers in the process. "He ate your crust," I said. It was true. Without even asking, he'd eaten the pizza crust that Mom left on her plate. And I'd have had to be blind to miss all the secret smiles they kept sharing. And what was with the peck on Mom's cheek when Jake dropped us off?

I felt my eyes well with tears. This was crazy. What was the big deal? It really *was* just pizza, and Jake really *was* a pretty cool guy. We both even liked mushrooms. I felt like the biggest baby in the universe.

Mom knelt beside me and touched my cheek. "Sweetie," she said, "I don't have to see him anymore. I didn't mean to upset you."

I shook my head, trying to shake the tears out of my eyes. "I'm not crying," I snapped, sniffling loudly. "Jake's nice. I don't mind if you go out again."

Mom took my brush from my hand, then put her arms around my neck. "Let's just take things nice and slow," she said. She pulled away from me and smiled. "Believe it or not, I'm not exactly irresistible."

I smiled. "You're definitely irresistible to Jake," I said.

"Yeah, well, *maybe* we'll squeeze him into our schedules occasionally or *maybe* we won't. I subtracted points for his messy car, so right now, he's in the minus column."

"*And* he ate your crust. You should subtract points for that."

"Absolutely. Even though I don't like crust. Just out of curiosity, does he get points for anything?"

I shrugged. "He didn't chop us up with an ax and put us

in the trunk of his car, so I guess he's not a serial killer. And we both like mushrooms."

Mom nodded. "Right. A non–serial killer who likes mushrooms. He should definitely get points for that."

See? It wasn't like I wasn't willing to give the guy a chance.

"The camera," Mom said solemnly, "is your friend."

"Hi, friend," I responded breezily, waving into the lens of the camcorder Mom held in front of me. It was Saturday afternoon, time for our crash course in broadcasting. Bridget had shown up at one o'clock sharp, early enough to scarf down a sandwich and chips with me before we got down to business.

"Pretend you're looking at a friend when you look into the lens," Mom instructed. "Eye contact. Erect but relaxed posture. Natural facial expressions. No fidgeting."

I cleared my throat and looked at the paper Bridget was holding beside Mom. We had printed out my essay in large type, and Bridge was doubling as a TelePrompTer.

"Reporting live from Crossroads Middle School, this is Talia Farrow with 'Talia Talk,' " I said.

"Why are you shouting at us?" Bridget asked.

"Sorry." I tugged at my shirt and repeated the line in a lowered voice.

"Now you're practically whispering," Mom said. "The key is to act natural. Talk in your normal tone of voice. Oh, and there's a glare, Bridget. Can you close the blinds?"

Bridget walked to the blinds in our family room and twisted the knob.

"Tilt your chin a little," she told me as she resumed her position. "You look like you're in a police lineup."

I flung my hands up. "How am I supposed to be natural with you two picking me apart?" I whined.

"You're supposed to *act* natural, not *be* natural," Mom corrected. "Let's try it again. 'Talia Talk,' take two."

"I think that's my line," Bridget said.

"Go for it."

" 'Talia Talk,' take two," Bridget said, and I broke into a nervous laugh.

"Cut! 'Talia Talk,' take three," Bridget said. "And . . . action!"

I read my essay off the cue cards, stumbling a couple of times but bouncing back without too much disruption. "Signing off for now, this is Talia Farrow for the Crossroads Oddcast," I concluded. I wrinkled my nose and shrugged.

"That was great, honey," Mom said, turning off the camcorder. "But slow down a little. And smile!"

I smiled.

"Not a blubbering-idiot smile," Bridget added hastily.

I pouted. "So I look like a blubbering idiot in a police lineup?"

"With peanut butter on your chin," Mom said, rubbing her own chin to show me where. "Sorry I didn't notice it before. But really, honey, you're doing fine."

I'd barely had time to rub the peanut butter off my chin when Bridget barked, " 'Talia Talk,' take four!"

"I'd rather take five," I groused.

"Not on my watch," Bridget responded coolly. "You've got to get your head in the game, Talia. We need to finish up so you can review the videotape while I go over my director's list with your mom. I've got tons of ideas: camera angles, split screens, aerial views of football games, a crawl for breaking news—"

"A *what?*" I asked.

"Crawl. The line that runs across the bottom of the screen on CNN."

"For breaking news like when the school secretary calls in sick?" Mom teased.

"Breaking news! Ms. Fishbein has a nosebleed!" I said as Mom and I doubled over laughing.

"People!" Bridget moaned. "We don't have all day, you know."

"Well, technically, we do," Mom said, and we both laughed harder.

Bridget tossed her head back and squeezed her eyes shut. "Amateurs."

I slammed my locker shut and slung my backpack over my shoulder.

"Wait up," Bridget called, hurrying down the hall to catch up with me. She broke into a trot, then ran up to me and pulled my hair band over my head.

"Bridget!" I groaned, glancing around to see if anyone was watching. I pushed the band back into place and smoothed my hair. "Ya mind?"

"I like it better the other way," Bridget said, then pulled it over my head again.

"*Bridget!*"

I straightened it again, feeling my shoulders tense and my face get warm.

She pretended to reach for it again. I slapped at her

hand, but she moved it at the last second. A cute guy walked by and rolled his eyes.

"Chill out!" I fumed, clenching my suddenly sweaty fists. "I'm already nervous about the auditions."

"Ooooh, the auditions, the auditions!" Bridget cooed. "Remember what we worked on: Relaxed posture. Eye contact. Natural tone of voice. No food on face. Got it?"

"I was thinking about smearing a banana on my nose."

"Yellow washes you out," Bridget said as we made our way to Ms. Stephens's room.

We stepped inside and I peered around anxiously.

My heart sank. Bridget and I had been acting like our spots on the Oddcast staff were practically a done deal, but at least two dozen sixth graders were milling around the room.

"Amateurs," Bridget whispered, cupping her mouth.

"That's the same thing you said about me when we were practicing," I reminded her.

The kids started taking seats. By the time they were settled, nearly every seat was filled. Bridget and I exchanged thumbs-up signs as we headed for opposite sides of the room for the only available seats left.

"Why do you hang out with her?"

I jumped at the sound of the voice, then turned to my right and realized I was sitting next to Meredith. Brynne sat behind her.

"Oh, hi," I said. "You're auditioning for the Oddcast?"

Meredith sat up straighter and adjusted her blouse. "No, the football team."

She exchanged glances with Brynne and snickered.

I let my backpack fall to the floor with a thud.

"I really don't get it," Meredith said. "Bridget is, like, the most annoying person on the planet. Why are you still hanging out with her?"

I blushed and stared at my fingers, which were clasped together on the desktop.

"If she were any louder, I'd need earplugs," Brynne said through gooey, peach-colored lips.

"It's not like she's the only person I ever hang out with . . . ," I said, twisting my fingers together.

Meredith's jaw dropped. "Other than every second of the day?"

"I mean, naturally we're friends," I murmured, "but I have lots of friends." I was still staring at my hands, which were growing sweatier by the second.

"Well, here's the thing," Meredith said. "I'm having a birthday party in a few weeks—a deejay, strobe lights, the whole deal—but it's by invitation only." She raised an eyebrow and Brynne leaned in close. "So if, like, I invited one person who I kinda wanted to come, but I didn't invite her BFF, who I definitely did *not* want to come, then—"

Brynne giggled into her fingertips.

"Then that would be cool?" Meredith asked, raising an eyebrow.

I opened my mouth, wondering what words would come out.

"Okay, guys, let's get started."

Whew. Ms. Stephens was starting the meeting.

"First, we'll go over the basics: don't bother auditioning if you're not willing to make a major commitment. Putting on a daily TV show, even if it's only five minutes long, takes a lot of work. Is everybody here up for three months of hard work?"

Bridget's hand shot into the air. Other hands went up slowly.

"Good," Ms. Stephens said. "If you take this seriously and put in the effort, you'll get a lot out of it. The Oddcast can be a ton of fun, and it's a great way to really become a part of your school. That's why we have sixth graders go first . . . kind of like boot camp for middle school. So: the Oddcast staff meets Thursdays after school for an hour. We report to school at seven-forty-five every morning, spending a few minutes going over scripts and setting up the camera. The show starts at eight a.m. sharp. We'll need four reporters and a camera operator—"

"Uh, Ms. Stephens?" Bridget said, hoisting her arm again. "I'll need an extra reporter, and at least two cameramen. *Videographer* is the technical term."

Ms. Stephens narrowed her eyes. *"You'll* need them?"

Bridget nodded. "As the director. *If* I'm named director, of course. I have a list of ideas."

Ms. Stephens leaned back against her desk. "And *if* you were named director," she said, "why might you need two cam—two videographers?"

"Remotes," Bridget said briskly. "I mean, it's a real thrill ride to see kids read announcements from behind a desk, but I'm thinking, let's go where the action is: basketball games, fire drills, cheerleading tryouts."

I slouched in my chair but noticed the other kids leaning toward Bridget, warming to her ideas.

Ms. Stephens smiled and held up her hand to quiet the class. "I like your enthusiasm, Bridget, but your ambitions might slightly outpace our capabilities."

"I like thinking big," Bridget replied.

"Let's think doable. We'll get our staff in place, then we'll ease into our routine."

Ben Angelo raised his hand. "I nominate Bridget as director," he said.

"Second!" Carl Brantley said from the desk behind Ben's.

Meredith sneered. "Oh. My. God," she huffed.

"Bridget's too bossy," I heard one kid murmur to another.

"Directors are supposed to be bossy," the other one replied.

Ms. Stephens made a time-out sign as murmurs rippled through the classroom. "Our staff isn't nominated," she said firmly. "It's assigned. By me. Bridget, you can show me your list at the end of the meeting. That goes for anyone else who wants to try out for director, too."

Her eyes scanned the room.

"Anyone? Anyone else trying out for director?"

"Too much work," one guy muttered.

"I live for work. So I'm in?" Bridget asked Ms. Stephens.

She smiled. "I can hardly wait to see your list. But now it's time for auditions for everyone trying out as an Oddcaster."

Most of the hands in the room shot up.

"That's what I thought," Ms. Stephens said breezily. "Everyone wants to be a star."

"Not me," Ben said. "I'm all about the camera work."

"You've got experience?" Bridget asked him.

"Well, I videotape my family's birthday parties."

"It's a start," Bridget replied. "We'll talk."

"Bridget!" Ms. Stephens moaned. "I'm in charge! And no one's made the staff yet."

"Right, Ms. Stephens," Bridget said with a wink.

Ms. Stephens rolled her eyes.

"Okay," she said, "everyone trying out for an Oddcaster spot, get in line, please."

Meredith, Brynne and I, along with about twenty other kids, settled into a line. We spent the next few minutes walking one at a time to the front of the classroom, where we held a sheet of announcements and read them to the class. Some kids' eyes never left the paper as they mumbled through the script. Others went all emo, making an announcement of library hours sound like a bulletin that a meteor had just smashed into the school. Some kids couldn't stop tugging on their clothes or biting their nails. A few girls (including Mer and Brynne, naturally) smiled and batted their lashes like *The Price Is Right* models. Cullen Bates got so nervous when he started his audition that he suddenly clutched his stomach and dove for the door.

Next was my turn.

I stood in front of the class, held the announcements in my hand and inhaled deeply. *Natural facial expressions. Relaxed posture. No fidgeting.*

"And the forecast today is mild and partly cloudy, with a high of eighty-three and a sixty-percent chance of rain," I concluded. "Hope you didn't forget an umbrella. Signing off for the Crossroads Oddcast, I'm Talia Farrow."

I paused, then looked nervously at Ms. Stephens. She glanced up from her notes, nodded at me with a smile and looked at the class.

"Girls and boys, Talia approached me a few days ago about the idea of adding a commentary to the Oddcast."

Bridget cleared her throat loudly.

"It was kind of Bridget's idea," I said softly.

"Would you mind reading your draft for the class? Let's see what they think about adding a commentary to the show."

Whoosh, whoosh, whoosh. That was the sound in my head. Pretty hard to ignore, except that I was distracted by the *boom, boom, boom* in my chest. My fingertips were sweaty as Ms. Stephens handed me the essay. My voice trembled as I began, but I caught Bridget's eyes and couldn't help smiling.

"So here are a few things I've learned so far that might help my fellow newbies," I read, hitting my stride.

I noticed the kids chuckling lightly as I continued my essay. I bounced on the balls of my feet—probably a strict violation of the "no fidgeting" rule, but I was too light-hearted to notice. This was really fun. And the kids were laughing. My essay couldn't be totally lame if they were laughing, right?

The kids laughed loudest at the friend amnesia part. Apparently, Brynne, Mer, Bridget and I had company in that arena.

"I'm sure I have lots more to learn, but that's all my brain can handle for now. Best of luck, fellow newbies. Signing off for now, this is Talia Farrow for the Crossroads Oddcast."

The students were smiling at me. A few even clapped lightly.

"Do you think that would make a nice weekly addition to the Oddcast?" Ms. Stephens asked them.

"I think it's a spectabulous idea," Bridget blurted.

And spectabulously enough, most of the class was nodding in agreement.

● ● ●

"So about the party . . ."

Ms. Stephens had wrapped up the Oddcast auditions, promising to post our names on the door the next morning if we made the staff. Bridget stayed behind to show Ms. Stephens her list of ideas. Meredith, Brynne and I gathered our backpacks as Meredith leaned in to whisper her reminder.

"The party?" I asked.

Meredith huffed. "The party I told you about twenty minutes ago, Einstein."

"She's registered at Threads," Brynne said breathlessly.

"Threads?"

"The coolest store in the mall," Brynne said. "Just to make it easier for people to know what to get her."

How thoughtful, I thought with an inward snicker.

"And even people who aren't invited can still check the registry and give her a present, so spread the word," Brynne continued.

Classic, I thought, trying to suppress my smirk.

"Definitely," Meredith said. "My registry's even posted on the Internet, so a couple of keystrokes and you're done."

"I'm going to register there for my party!" Brynne gushed.

Meredith slung her backpack over her shoulder. "So," she said to me, "I'll give you an invitation?"

"Um, sure. Why not?"

I walked out and sighed with relief when I saw my grandpa waiting for me in the school parking lot. I opened the door, slung my backpack into the backseat and fastened my seat belt as I sat down.

"How was school, missy?" Grandpa asked.

"Okay," I said. "We just had Oddcast auditions. I think I did pretty well."

"When will you know if you made it?" he asked.

"Tomorrow."

"Well, I think you're a shoo-in." He tapped the steering wheel and hummed as he pulled out of the parking lot.

"Grandma's got spaghetti cooking," he said. "Dinner at our place sound okay tonight?"

That was weird. We ate at Grandma and Grandpa's a lot on weekends, but usually not during the week. "Is Mom coming?" I asked.

Grandpa shook his head. "No, she's eating out with a friend tonight."

My eyes narrowed. "Jake?"

Grandpa's eyes followed the road. "That okay?" he asked.

"Sure. Why wouldn't it be?" There were those stomach knots again.

Grandpa drove in silence for a few minutes, then quickly opened his mouth to say something but shut it. A minute later, he tried again. "You know, for years, your grandma and I have been trying to talk your mom into dating," he said. I swallowed hard. "That might sound odd; after all, your dad was our son. But your mother's like a daughter to us, and we want her to be happy. And she is happy—no doubt about it—but she's got her whole life ahead of her, and we think she could squeeze a nice fella into that life, if she would just give somebody a chance."

He glanced at me from the corner of his eye, but I stared straight ahead. "So Grandma and I, we're tickled that she's willing to spend a little time with a friend. No telling what will come of it—they're just friends, after all—but we think it's a good thing." He paused. "How about you?"

Trees passed by my window in a blur. "Whatever," I said.

Grandpa stopped at a red light and turned to face me. "Talia, you're the most important person in your mother's life. If you're not happy, she's not happy."

What was that supposed to mean? "It's *fine* that she's having dinner with Jake, okay?" I snapped. "Geez! Are they eloping or something? Why are you making this seem like such a big deal? It's dinner, for crying out loud."

Grandpa was silent.

My face softened. "Sorry I snapped at you." He reached for my hand and I squeezed it. "Spaghetti sounds really good."

More trees passed by in a blur. "Grandpa," I said, staring dreamily out the window, "if you had a best friend who you totally loved—*totally*—but who was acting all goofy and annoying at school, making your other friends kinda avoid her . . ."

My voice trailed off. More blurry trees, plus a few blurry kids walking on sidewalks with their blurry backpacks.

"Are we supposing that my hypothetical best friend has always been goofy and annoying?" Grandpa asked. "Or are we supposing that my best friend has changed?"

Good question. "We're supposing that she's always been goofy and annoying. We're supposing it's everybody else who has changed. The people who used to think she was really fun and funny now think she's irritating and immature. Would you keep hanging out with a friend like that?"

What a horrible question. How could I even consider dumping Bridget?

Grandpa scratched his head with one hand while he steered with the other. "I'm a pretty loyal friend," he said after a long pause. "If someone is a good friend to me, I'm not likely to care if other people suddenly turn against him. In fact, that's when my loyalty really kicks in. If *I* have a reason to doubt his character or his friendship, that's one thing. But what other people think doesn't really wash with me."

I bit my lower lip. "But what if they kinda have a point?"

Grandpa nodded. "Oh, so you're saying that the reason they turned against this person is because she's not such a nice person anymore."

"No, not at all," I said quickly. "Your friend's great. She'd give anybody the shirt off her back. She's just loud and embarrassing sometimes."

Grandpa narrowed his eyes and looked at me sideways. "I'm loud and embarrassing sometimes. You wanna dump me?"

I giggled. "No way. I love you just the way you are."

He nodded slowly, staring ahead as he drove. "Yup," he said. "I guess that's the definition of friendship in a nutshell."

The phone was ringing when I got home from Grandma and Grandpa's house that evening. Mom fiddled quickly with her keys so she could unlock the door. I ran in ahead of her and answered the phone. "Hello?"

"Where ya been?"

"Hi, Bridget. My mom had a . . . thing tonight, so I ate dinner with Grandma and Grandpa. She picked me up a few minutes ago and we just got home."

"A thing? What's a thing?"

Nothing slipped past Bridget.

I carried my cordless phone into my room, shut the door behind me and plopped on my bed as I talked. "It's weird," I said in a hushed voice. "I think she's kinda got a boyfriend."

Bridget gasped. "No way!"

I shook my head quickly. "Not really a boyfriend," I

qualified. "Just a friend. His name is Jake. They had dinner. And they took me out for pizza the other night."

"Your mom has a *boyfriend?*" She made the word sound like a disease.

I rolled my eyes. "A friend who's a boy. Well, a man. Or a guy. Whatever. He's pretty cool. I think they just like hanging out."

"Adults don't hang out," Bridget said. "They date and then get married. Omigod, Talia, you're gonna have a stepfather!"

I groaned. "Tonight was their first real date!"

"Yeah, but the fact that your mom wanted you two to meet each other before they had a real date . . . she must have it bad."

I squinched my face in frustration. " 'Have it bad'? She's my mother, Bridget, not a rock-star groupie."

"What are you gonna wear to the wedding?"

I couldn't help but laugh. Grandpa was right about friendship. Who cared what anybody else thought? Bridget always made me laugh.

"Talia, I have to check this guy out," Bridget continued. "Maybe do a background check or something. Do you think you could get a DNA sample without being too obvious? Like maybe a piece of his hair?"

I was still chuckling. "Yeah, I'm pretty subtle about plucking out people's hair."

"Ooooh, idea, idea!" Bridget cooed. "This can be your first Oddcast commentary. Rat out your mom about her new boyfriend!"

I frowned. "I could never do that to my poor mom. She'd die."

75

"Oh, like you didn't die when she told the whole world about your crush on the paperboy?"

Good point.

"Or like you didn't die when she talked about you trying to stick antlers on your head with bubble gum for Christmas?"

"Stop reminding me of all those things. You'll activate my anxiety rash."

"You're right. We should reserve our ammo for Mer and Brynne. You can tell the whole school Mer split her shorts at the baseball game last spring when she was doing a cartwheel trying to impress Todd Baisden." Bridget giggled. "Remember the look on her face when she realized everybody was staring at her solar-system underpants? I called her Pluto for a month."

I rolled my eyes. "First of all, you're assuming we'll make the Oddcast staff."

"Oh, we're in, girlfriend, we're in."

"*Second,*" I said, "you're assuming Ms. Stephens will let me do a commentary."

"Goes without saying. It's a brilliant idea."

"And *third,* you're assuming Ms. Stephens, who has to approve all the Oddcast copy, would let me talk about Meredith's split shorts to the whole school."

"Good point," Bridget said. "Dicey, but manageable. We'll just tell all without using actual names. You know, 'Students, today I'd like to talk about ways *not* to impress boys at baseball games. One: Skip the cartwheels if your shorts are painted on. Two: If your shorts are painted on and you do cartwheels anyhow, plan it that you're wearing respectable-looking underpants.' Get it? Plan it? Planet?"

I giggled and shook my head. "I need to do my homework. Bye, Bridget. Beam back down to planet Earth in time for school tomorrow."

13

About a dozen kids were already crowded around the Oddcast list when I reached Ms. Stephens's door first thing the next morning. Meredith and Brynne were at the front of the line, squealing and jumping up and down.

"Think they made it?" Ben Angelo teased as I burrowed my head closer.

"Coming through, coming through!"

It was Bridget, speed-walking down the hall as she approached Ms. Stephens's door. "Are we in? Are we in?" she asked as she reached my side. *We.* I was always a *we* with Bridget.

"I dunno. I can't see the list yet," I said, rising to my tiptoes for a better view.

By this time, Ben had inched close enough to see the list. "You're in," he told me.

"Really?"

"Okay, guys, I'll read the list out loud if that will keep you from squishing me," Meredith said. "The Oddcast staff is me, Brynne, Carl Brantley, David McNair, Shelley Grayson, Ben Angelo and Talia Farrow."

My heart skipped a beat. No Bridget?

"Oh, and Bridget," Meredith added grudgingly.

I bounced on my toes. "We're in! We're in!"

"Does it have me down for director?" Bridget asked Meredith.

Mer planted a hand on her hip. "Look, just because you're the director doesn't mean you get to always have your way and boss everybody around."

"I'm the director!" Bridget grabbed my hands and spun me around, knocking me into Ben.

"Bridget!" I scolded, tossing Ben an apologetic glance.

The crowd started thinning as kids who hadn't made the cut lowered their heads and walked away. Poor guys. I knew the feeling from powder-puff cheerleading tryouts, fourth-grade volleyball tryouts, fifth-grade election for class officers. . . . The list went on.

"This is the first time I've ever won anything," I gushed to Bridget, then noticed Ms. Stephens had walked up.

"You didn't *win* it, you *earned* it," Ms. Stephens said. "Congratulations, Oddcast staff."

"Ms. Stephens, I'd like to start a fashion report for the Oddcast," Meredith said, raising her hand.

"Me too!" Brynne echoed.

Ms. Stephens waved her hands to calm everybody down. "Our first meeting is Thursday after school," she said.

"We'll plan on launching the Oddcast next week, assuming we're ready. Right now, it's time to get to class."

"A fashion report?" Bridget asked me with a snicker as we walked toward Ms. Perkins's class. "Can she start by blending in her blush?"

"You're a total laugh riot," Meredith snapped, overhearing. "Just remember: you don't get to make all the rules."

"Yeah, Bridget," Brynne chimed in. "Don't forget the tug-of-war."

Bridget rolled her eyes. "What does the tug-of-war have to do with anything?"

"If I remember correctly, you're the one who ended up covered in mud," Brynne replied.

"So you're threatening to pull me into the mud?"

Meredith smiled at Brynne and raised an eyebrow. "Not a bad idea."

● ● ●

"So," I said as I swallowed a bite of my chicken sandwich in the cafeteria, "think we'll be ready for our first Oddcast next week?"

Bridget bounced in her seat. "Oh, we'll be ready. Ben and I have already started brainstorming. We're going to do person-on-the-street interviews when people are changing classes. You know, like, 'What do you consider to be Ms. Perkins's most unfortunate facial feature?'"

I giggled.

"And we're staying after school shooting footage of different activities. We'll be shooting the cheerleaders tomorrow. Shooting cheerleaders: I like the sound of that. Uh-oh. Speaking of which . . . ," she said in a lowered voice, looking over my shoulder.

"Hi, Talia," Meredith said as she and Brynne reached our table. "Um, we're sitting at that table over there." She motioned with her head toward the other side of the cafeteria. "You can sit with us if you want. The thing is, there's only one extra seat."

She tossed Bridget a fake smile.

"No problem," Bridget said with a mouth full of salad. "I'll sit on Talia's lap. Let's go, Talia. That side of the cafeteria looks way cooler than this side. I think that side has designer linoleum."

Meredith and Brynne rolled their eyes. "Whatever," Meredith said. "I was just offering to be nice. So, sit where you want, Talia."

My eyes darted from Bridget to Meredith and back again.

"Um . . . ," I said, licking my lips, "we've already started eating, so I'm good. But thanks for asking. Maybe tomorrow?"

I could feel Bridget's eyes boring into me, but I kept my focus on Meredith.

"Whatever," Meredith said. "And don't forget about the . . . the . . ." She cast an annoyed glance at Bridget. "The *event* I mentioned in Ms. Stephens's room yesterday."

"Right," I mumbled.

"Well, see ya," Meredith said, and she and Brynne walked to the opposite side of the cafeteria.

Bridget was still staring me down as I gazed at my macaroni and cheese.

" 'Maybe tomorrow'?" she asked me accusingly.

"What?" I said, pretending I hadn't quite been following the conversation.

"Maybe tomorrow you'll sit with the Snob Squad?"

I waved my hand through the air. "I was just being nice," I said, hurrying to take another bite so my mouth would be full.

Bridget paused, still studying my face. "So will you sit with them tomorrow, just to be nice?"

I chewed extra long to keep my mouth occupied. But Bridget was willing to wait me out. I had no choice but to swallow. "What's the big deal?" I said, still avoiding eye contact. "We can sit here, we can sit there . . . whatever."

Bridget's eyebrows crinkled together. "No, *you* can sit here or *you* can sit there. I wasn't invited."

I put my fork down and gritted my teeth. "Nobody was *invited*," I said, trying to sound annoyed. "They just said an extra chair was at their table, in case anybody wanted to sit in it."

"In case *you* wanted to sit in it," Bridget said, emphasizing every word. "And what 'event' was Meredith talking about? Did she invite you to a party or something?"

I rolled my eyes. "As *if*."

Bridget shook her head slowly. "You are such a suck-up."

I felt my face flush. "Then why do you want to hang around me?"

Bridget's shoulders stiffened. "Maybe I don't."

"You're not exactly nice to them either, you know," I reminded her. "Making fun of their makeup? Even when we were all friends, you used to rag on them. Remember Mer's underpants? *Pluto?*"

Bridget's jaw dropped. "You were laughing just as hard as I was!"

"Maybe I shouldn't have been. *Meredith* wasn't laughing."

Bridget's eyes narrowed into slits. "Meredith and Brynne laugh at me *every day*. Or haven't you noticed? I was a great friend to them until they started dissing me. I guess I'm funny that way, not liking friends to treat me like garbage."

"Maybe if you didn't embarrass us so much . . ."

Time froze as Bridget's eyes locked with mine. Finally, she said in a steely voice, "Consider it done."

She stood up and walked to another table.

My stomach knotted as I stared into my macaroni and cheese. I picked at it a couple of times, but the fork never made it to my mouth. Bridget was so infuriating! Why was she making me feel this way? Why did I have to choose between friends? It was so unfair!

I slammed my fork on my plate. "*She's* the one who left," I muttered to myself, which made it perfectly logical to do what I did next.

I went and sat with Mer and Brynne.

14

"And the forms for parent volunteers are due Monday," Brynne said into the camera from the teachers' conference room, which doubled as our Oddcast studio.

Brynne sat behind the conference table with the other reporters and me, facing Ms. Stephens, Bridget and Ben Angelo, who was operating the camcorder.

Today's after-school meeting was doubling as our dress rehearsal, our last chance to practice before presenting our debut Oddcast the next morning.

"Cut," Bridget barked as Brynne continued her part of the script. "You're overenunciating."

Ben turned off the camcorder and Brynne held up the palms of her hands. "Huh?" Brynne said.

"O-ver-e-*nun*-ci-a-ting."

Brynne pouted at Ms. Stephens. "Does Bridget get to

boss us around just because she's the director? She's more like a dictator."

Ms. Stephens shrugged. "Bridget's right; your speech patterns sound a little forced. Just relax and be natural. Act like you're sharing the information with a friend."

"And one who's not hard of hearing," Bridget added.

Brynne read her lines again, more naturally this time.

"Much better," Ms. Stephens said. "Let's move on to Talia. Talia, are you ready for your first commentary tomorrow?"

I sucked in my bottom lip. "I guess."

I reached into my backpack, pulled out the essay I'd drafted the first day of school, smoothed it on the table and cleared my throat. I started reading, making sure to look into the camera every few seconds like Mom had taught me. Ben was smiling at me from behind the camcorder. My voice trembled at first, then grew firmer.

"But here are a few things I've learned so far that might help my fellow newbies," I read. "One: Locker combinations are trickier than they look—"

"*Cut!*" Bridget groaned.

"What?" I asked.

"You can't use the same essay you wrote two weeks ago," Bridget responded. "I think 'the newbies' have had time to figure out their locker combinations by now, don't you think?"

I blushed. Bridget had avoided me since our spat in the lunchroom. It suited me fine. *She* was the one who'd walked away. *She* was the one who couldn't take a little constructive criticism. Granted, it was getting a little boring spending

85

lunch periods listening to Meredith talk about her Threads registry, but at least she and Brynne didn't embarrass me to death. Besides, Bridget had been spending lunch periods shooting footage with Ben and Shelley, the Oddcast videographers. It was a relief to have a little space. Being joined at the hip with Bridget was exhausting.

"Ms. Stephens, tell Talia she has to write a new essay," Bridget said in a clipped tone.

"I think the essay still works," Ms. Stephens said.

"*Not!*" Bridget wailed. "It's *so* two weeks ago. Talia's had all this time to write something new."

"Which I would have happily done, if anyone had told me I needed to," I said through gritted teeth.

"Consider yourself told," Bridget said icily.

Mer and Brynne twittered beside me. Ben shut off his camcorder and let out a low whistle.

"You're not my boss, Bridget," I said evenly.

"I'm the director." Bridget jutted out her chin. "Step up or step off."

We glared at each other for a long moment.

"Girls!" The urgency in Ms. Stephens's voice startled us out of our showdown. "What's going on with you two? You're best friends!"

"Bridget's too bossy!" Brynne sputtered, nodding sharply.

"Way too bossy," Meredith said. "Talia, your essay's just fine."

"I think Bridget should be fired!" Brynne said.

I sucked in my breath. Bridget crossed her arms and turned toward the wall. Silence hung in the air.

"No way," Ben said quietly. "She's an incredible director.

We've been shooting footage every day, including after school. She interviewed Coach Quinn about the football season and asked really good questions. The football team said it was the only time they'd heard him speak more than two words at once."

"She even got the football players to do a cheerleader pyramid," Shelley added. "It was hilarious."

"We'll have the most awesome Oddcast ever, if you'll let her do her job," Ben said.

I stared at Bridget's back, not sure whether I wanted to comfort her or strangle her.

"I think Bridget's right," I finally said in a small voice. "I'll write a new essay."

Ms. Stephens set her jaw. "Guys," she said, "we're a team. We stand or we fall *as a team*. I don't expect everyone on the staff to be best friends, but I do expect mutual support and respect." She paused and gazed at every face. "If you can't manage that, this is a good time to bail out. We work too closely together to be petty."

Meredith sneered, and Ms. Stephens looked at her sharply. "And Bridget is the director," she said, still holding Mer's gaze. "But that doesn't mean her word is law. I have the final say about everything. But it means she has a lot of responsibility. And Ben's right: she's doing a fantastic job."

"She's still too bossy," Meredith grumbled under her breath.

Ms. Stephens looked at me. "Talia, it's up to you: do you think you can have a new essay ready in the morning in time for me to review it?"

I nodded uneasily.

"Good. Bring your original draft, too, just in case there's any problem with the new one. Let's wrap it up for today and come back in the morning, *as a team*. Seven-forty-five sharp. We've got a show to put on."

We sat there awkwardly for a minute, then began stuffing our papers into our backpacks. Bridget was the first to walk out the door. Impulsively, I grabbed my backpack and hurried to catch up with her.

"Wait up," I called as we reached the hall. She didn't slow down.

"Bridget!"

I quickened my pace and walked beside her.

"Why are you being so awful to me?" I asked breathlessly, shifting the weight of my backpack.

"Sorry you and the Snob Squad couldn't manage to get me fired," she said, still looking straight ahead. "Better luck next time."

I squeezed my eyes shut, then popped them open. "If you'll *recall*," I sputtered, "I'm the one who defended you!"

"My bad," Bridget said coolly. "I could have sworn that was Ben. Do you get that a lot? People confusing you with Ben?"

I huffed. "What do you want from me? I agreed to write another essay. Thanks for that, by the way. Twelve hours' notice is totally sufficient."

Bridget stopped in her tracks and turned to face me. "Who knew you were still planning to talk about locker combinations? How lame can you get? Granted, I'm the brains of the organization, but do I have to tell you everything?"

Tears sprang to my eyes.

Bridget sighed. Her face softened. "I'd love it if we'd had a chance to talk about it earlier," she said. "But you weren't talking to me."

I rolled my eyes. "*You* weren't talking to *me!*"

"It's one thing for Brynne and Mer to treat me like dryer lint," Bridget said, now on the verge of tears herself. "It's another for *you* to."

I looked at her pleadingly. "I haven't been avoiding you," I said, but I couldn't quite look her in the eye. "You've been so busy with the Oddcast. And Ben's right: you're doing an awesome job. Just imagine what everybody will think when they're expecting boring announcements, and the next thing they know, they're watching the football players in a cheerleader pyramid. You're amazing."

Bridget blinked back tears and smiled weakly. "If I could write like you, I wouldn't have to stay after school interviewing football coaches. Want me to help you with your essay?"

I raised an eyebrow. "Considering you're the reason I'm stuck with this assignment, I think that's an excellificent idea."

15

Our sneakers padded in unison as we made our way down the hall, then out the door to the parking lot, where Grandpa was waiting.

"You pretty girls need a lift, by any chance?" Grandpa teased as we dumped our backpacks into the trunk of his car.

"I dunno, Mr. Farrow. My mom told me not to accept rides with strange men, and you're pretty strange," Bridget teased back.

"You've never held it against me before," he said.

"Good point," Bridget said. "Onward."

I kissed Grandpa spontaneously on the cheek. Why hadn't I listened to his advice about friendship? Oh, well. Now that Bridget and I were together again, it was like we'd never been apart.

She leaned toward the front seat. "What's the latest with your mom's new boyfriend?" she asked me.

Grandpa drew in his breath. "Her new *what?*"

"Boyfriend," Bridget repeated. "Talia told me all about him."

Grandpa's neck reddened. "He's just a friend, that's all."

I giggled. "Grandpa, give it up. The whole 'just a friend' spiel is getting a little old."

"He *is* just a friend," Grandpa insisted.

"A friend who's totally nuts about Mom. It's okay. I'm cool with it." I rolled down my window and let my hair blow in the breeze.

"So is it weird for your mom to have a boyfriend?" Bridget asked.

I shrugged. "Kinda."

"Is he like your dad?"

Grandpa and I exchanged glances. That was Bridget, just blurting out whatever she was thinking. But I didn't mind. "Dad's hair was more blondish," I said.

"And more baldish," Grandpa said, squeezing my knee.

"I mean his personality," Bridget clarified. "What was he like? I can barely remember."

I looked at Grandpa. He winked.

"Um . . . I remember he liked to sing," I said, squinting into the wind blowing in my face. "He used to sing to me all the time. They were real songs, but he'd put my name in the words: '*Lovely Talia, meter maid. . . .*' Stuff like that. And Dad was funny."

Grandpa nodded. "He could tell a story like nobody's

business. Our favorite was about the night you were born. We asked him to tell that story again and again, and we laughed just as hard every time. Seems he and your mom were in the middle of a Scrabble game when she went into labor, and they were both so competitive, they didn't want to stop the game. So they took it to the hospital, your dad balancing the Scrabble board to keep the tiles in place—you'd have to hear him tell it—and him winning the game just a few minutes before you were born, adding the letters T, A, L and I to an A in your mother's *AARDVARK.*"

I squinted into the wind blowing in my face. "In the first place," I said, playing along even though I'd heard the story a million times before, "you can't use a proper name in Scrabble. In the second place, Mom should have won on general principle considering she knew how to spell *aardvark.* Not to mention that she was in labor. And in the third place, naming me after a Scrabble word is beyond tacky. What if Dad's tiles had spelled out *amnesia?*"

Grandpa chuckled, his eyes sparkling.

"What did your dad do for a living?" Bridget asked me.

"He was an actuary," Grandpa responded. Bridget's eyebrows wrinkled together, but I held up my hand to stop her question.

"It's a boring answer," I assured her.

"But your dad was no boring guy," Grandpa said, then added in almost a whisper, "He was my boy."

"Well," I said, "I'm just glad his tiles spelled out *something.* Otherwise, I guess my name would have been Aardvark."

We drove in silence for a few seconds; then Bridget said, "What's the latest on Meredith's blowout birthday party?"

I squirmed. "Huh?" I asked, as if I'd barely been paying attention.

"A party, eh?" Grandpa said. "You girls invited?"

"Talia probably is," Bridget said, looking to me for verification, but I stared straight ahead.

"She's spent the whole week making this big show of 'subtly' handing out her invitations to the A-list," Bridget told Grandpa. "Guess who didn't make the cut."

"Not you!" Grandpa teased, feigning astonishment.

"Tragic yet true. And she tried to get me fired today as the Oddcast director."

"Is this the same Meredith you girls used to always run around with? She and the brunette . . . Brawn, is it?"

Bridget and I laughed. "Brynne, Grandpa," I said. "Yes, that's the same Meredith."

"So why aren't you all friends anymore?" he asked.

"Talia's their friend," Bridget responded.

"I *so* am not!"

"You *so* are too," Bridget said with the slightest edge in her voice.

"I've just been sitting with them in the cafeteria because Bridget blew me off," I explained to Grandpa.

"You're going to Mer's party, aren't you?" Bridget asked me.

"Did you hear she's registered at Threads?" I asked with a conspiratorial grin. "Oh, and good news: Even the people who aren't invited are still allowed to buy her a present.

See? She's no snob. She wants everybody to have the pleasure of buying her a gift."

Bridget buried her face in her hands laughing. I chuckled, too, but I noticed Grandpa eyeing me warily. "Maybe we should take up a collection at school: Help Keep Meredith in Cashmere," I said, making Bridget laugh harder.

Sorry, Grandpa, I thought, knowing how he felt about gossip. I hated to disappoint him.

But it felt so good to be laughing with Bridget again.

● ● ●

Bridget put a hand on a hip as she peered skeptically at our creation.

"Looks mushy in the middle."

It was her idea to bake one giant chocolate chip cookie rather than a bunch of regular-sized cookies, despite my warning that cookie dough wasn't meant to be smushed into a cake pan.

But she'd insisted.

"Bridget, do you have to be different just for the sake of being different?"

"I have to be different for the sake of being magnificent," she responded.

Of course, as soon as we took the cake pan out of the oven, we both knew I was right.

"It's not cooked in the middle," I said. "And it's burned on the sides. I told you we should've just made regular cookies."

Mom walked into the kitchen, wrinkling her nose. "What's burning?"

"Bridget's cookie cake," I said.

"My cookie cake? You're the one who mixed the batter," Bridget said.

"You're the one who put it in the cake pan. And you put too much dough in the middle."

"I wanted it to look like a cookie mountain."

Mom waved her hand in front of her face to clear the burning smell. "Mount Mush?" she suggested.

"Mount Magnificent," Bridget said. "Want a piece?"

"Gee, as tempting as that sounds, I think I'll pass. I thought you girls were working on a project."

"My Oddcast essay. I finished a few minutes ago," I said.

Mom's face brightened. "Can I read it?"

Bridget and I sneaked glances and stifled giggles. "I'd rather you be surprised," I said.

"O-*kay*," Mom said warily. "So who else is on the Oddcast staff? Anyone I know?"

"Mer and Brynne," Bridget said.

"Oh, good!" Mom gushed. "The Four Musketeers are together again."

Bridget shook her head. "Our friendship is so five minutes ago," she said. "Mer's snob quotient is off the charts. She's having some big froufrou birthday party, and you'd think she was the Queen of England."

"Are you girls invited?" Mom asked.

"Talia is," Bridget said.

"Just because I'm invited doesn't mean I'm going," I

clarified, dabbing my finger in the cookie cake, then yanking it away when the tip burned.

Mom shook her head. "She used to be such a sweet girl . . ."

A horn blared from the driveway. "My mom," Bridget said. "Gotta go."

"What about Mount Magnificent?" I said.

"It's all yours," Bridget said. "I just create brilliance. I leave it to the masses to enjoy it. And clean up!"

"Gee, thanks."

She scooped up her backpack, reminded me to be at school the next morning at seven-forty-five sharp, then zipped out the door.

I waved, then answered the ringing phone in the kitchen. "Hello?"

"Can you believe her?" Meredith hissed on the other end.

" 'Her'?"

"Bridget! I don't think I can stand three months of her telling me what to do. Why wouldn't Ms. Stephens fire her like we begged her to?"

I shoved a hand into my jeans pocket. "She *is* working really hard on the Oddcast. . . ."

"Uh, hello? Looks like she's making you do all the work. A new essay, one day before the first Oddcast? Look, Talia, I admire you for trying to stick by her and all—I mean, you're the only one left on the planet who can stand her, except for a few brainiacs like Ben—but you've got to cut her loose. She's no friend. She was, like, totally snotty to you at the meeting."

"Yeah, she kinda was. . . ."

"I think we should make a petition to fire her as direc-tor. If enough people sign it, Ms. Stephens will *have* to pay attention."

Subject change. Subject change.

"Everything all set for your party?" I asked, trying to sound casual.

"What?" Meredith asked. "Of course. You're coming, aren't you?"

"Uh . . ."

"All the cute guys will be there, Talia. This is your chance to make your break. Otherwise, your reputation is sealed: Loser Bridget's Best Friend."

"Yeah, well . . . I've got to ask my mom if I can go. I'll call you right back, okay?"

I sighed with relief as we said goodbye, only to feel my muscles tighten as I hung up the phone and noticed Mom standing there.

"Was that Meredith?" she asked cautiously.

"Who? Oh, right. Meredith. Yeah."

Mom squeezed her lips together. "I thought you told Bridget you weren't going to her party."

I flung a hand into the air. "Who said I was going? And who said I *wasn't* going? I don't recall actually saying that. And why does everybody care so much whether I go to a stupid party?"

Mom shifted her weight and crossed her arms. "Honey," she said, "I'm not trying to tell you whether to go to a party or not—and I'm certainly not trying to tell you who your friends should be—but you wouldn't be playing both ends against the middle, would you?"

I swallowed hard. "What do you mean?"

"I mean you were snickering about Meredith with Bridget, and now it seems like you're talking about Bridget to Meredith."

"Meredith called *me*," I reminded her testily. "And Bridget's the one who was making fun of Meredith. I'm just trying to be nice to everybody, but it doesn't seem to matter what I do, because I keep getting grief everywhere I turn, and all I want is for everybody to be friends like we used to be."

Mom nodded. "So . . . do you want to go to Meredith's party?"

My shoulders sank. "Meredith really has turned into Little Miss All-That. But I wouldn't totally hate the idea of hanging around with a few people besides just Bridget. And *everybody* will be at Meredith's party."

Mom bit her lower lip. "Not Bridget."

"Well, everybody cool," I said, then sucked in my breath, wishing I could take it back.

"Talia," Mom said, "it's one thing to go to a snob's birthday party. It's another thing to *be* a snob."

"I am not a snob! But it's supposed to be a really fun party with a deejay and strobe lights and . . . why are you looking at me that way?"

Mom's eyes softened. "I didn't say you shouldn't go, honey. You know I've always liked Meredith. Maybe she's just going through a phase. It happens sometimes when kids get really preoccupied with what other people think of them."

"Meredith doesn't worry about what other people think

of her," I said. "Other people worry about what she thinks of *them*."

Mom gently took my hand. "I bet Bridget doesn't. And I wouldn't think you would, either."

"Look," I told Mom, "all I'm saying is: There's a party a week from Saturday and I'm invited. I'm supposed to RSVP. I kinda want to go and I kinda don't. I can't help who's invited and who's not. So that's the deal." I looked at her pleadingly. "What do you think I should do?"

Mom shook her head. "I don't have all the answers, honey." She sighed. "I think," she finally said, "that this is your call to make. Pun intended."

She tossed her head in the direction of the phone.

It was time to RSVP.

16

I knew what it felt like to have butterflies in my stomach. But as I listened to Brynne making the Oddcast announcements, then David giving the weather forecast, then Carl doing the sports interspersed with Bridget's football-practice footage, my butterflies seemed to transform into crazed killer wasps set on devouring my internal organs. I dug my fingernails into my palms and bit my bottom lip.

Not only had my insides turned to jelly, but I *looked* like a schlumpy mess, too. Bridget and I had decided to wear our Otters camp T-shirts for solidarity (well, actually, it was *her* idea), but now I was having big-time second thoughts. My T-shirt combined with my limp ponytail made me look like I'd crawled out from under a rock. This compared to Mer and Brynne, all camera-ready in their matching pastel sweater sets and sleekly straightened hair. What was I thinking? Meredith's fashion report was starting to seem like a good idea. I could use some help.

And speaking of help, Ms. Stephens said she liked my new essay, but was she just being polite? Was it totally stupid? If so, I was about to make a supersized fool of myself. Why couldn't I be content to just read the announcements? *Bridget*, that's why. Every time I found myself way over my head, all roads led back to Bridget.

Speaking of . . .

I took a deep breath as I noticed Bridget from the corner of my eye, doing a countdown on her fingers, mouthing the numbers as she went along. *"Five, four, three . . ."* Uh-oh. Ready or not, it was time for my first Oddcast commentary.

As Bridget's last finger curled down to her hand, Ben turned the camera toward me in my seat next to Shelley's. Was it possible for a heart to explode? I was about to find out.

"Reporting live from Crossroads Middle School, this is Talia Farrow with 'Talia Talk,' a new weekly commentary for the Oddcast.

"You heard Brynne mention that Monday is the deadline for us to turn in parent volunteer forms, and that got me to thinking."

Breathe, Talia, breathe. Inhale, already.

"As you know, the forms give a list of volunteer opportunities at school so the parents can sign up if they want to."

I saw Bridget stretching out her hands in the corner of my eye. *"Slow down,"* she was mouthing. *"Slow down."*

"Okay, I'll admit it," I said slowly. "I've put off giving the form to my mom until the last minute. The problem isn't that I think she *won't* sign up. The problem is that I know she *will*."

Bridget was making a stirring motion with her hand. "*Speed up,*" she mouthed. "*Speed up.*" God! No pressure there.

"We all know the type: the moms who volunteer for everything, especially if it has anything to do with our education," I said a little bit faster but not too fast. *Breathe.* "I'd like to educate these moms about how to be a good school volunteer. The short version: Everything you normally do, do the opposite." The Oddcast staff chuckled. I inhaled deeper and continued.

"The biggest problem is that mom volunteers are way too perky. Every time my mom comes to school, she has a big smile pasted on her face and waves to all the kids, calling them by name.

"Note I didn't say calling them by *their* names, because she usually gets them wrong. I've gone to school with a guy named Peter since kindergarten and Mom calls him Caleb. No, Caleb isn't his middle name. No, Caleb isn't the name of his identical twin brother—he doesn't have one. There's no reason at all to call him Caleb, but that name is stuck in my mom's head. He just smiles politely when she calls him that. What's the point of correcting her after all these years?

"Mom-volunteer perkiness spills over in other ways too. My mom likes to chat with my classmates, which I wouldn't necessarily mind if the conversations were halfway

102

interesting. Sadly, no such luck. So when she's driving a carload of kids to a museum for a field trip, for instance, she'll ask them one by one what their parents do for a living or what their favorite subject is. The kids are always sneaking me frantic looks while they're answering her questions, like they're thinking, *When is my interview over? And why does your mom care that my dad is an accountant?* It's like being chaperoned by the CIA."

The Oddcast staff chuckled again. I noticed my heart wasn't pounding through my chest anymore.

"I know mom volunteers mean well, but I can't help wondering: would it be so terrible if I accidentally forgot to show my mom this form?

"I'm thinking 'Caleb' would vote no.

"Signing off for now, this is Talia Farrow for the Crossroads Oddcast."

Bridget mouthed *"Cut."* Ben turned off the camcorder. I blinked hard and came up for air for the first time in three minutes.

"Great job!" Ms. Stephens said, her eyes twinkling.

"Ms. Stephens, could I double as a makeup artist?" Meredith asked. "I didn't get many lines in the Oddcast anyway. I might as well put my talents to use by making sure everybody looks halfway professional."

She wrinkled her nose as she looked at Bridget's and my T-shirts. I tugged at mine self-consciously.

"Mer, considering you have a piece of bacon stuck between your teeth, I'm not sure you qualify as an authority," Bridget said.

"Omigod!" Meredith slapped her hand over her mouth.

"I was kidding," Bridget groaned. "You think I'd let you on the air with food in your teeth?"

Meredith's eyes narrowed. "You are the worst director ever!"

Bridget took a bow.

"Settle down, guys," Ms. Stephens said. "It's time to get to your first-period class. Be here at seven-forty-five Monday morning for the next Oddcast. I'll have a script ready to go . . . lower-maintenance next time, with just announcements. We'll let Fridays be our pull-out-the-stops day. Keep up the good work."

As we filtered out of the room, Ms. Stephens gently pulled my arm. "You're a natural, Talia," she said. "Can you have your next commentary written by Thursday?"

I blushed. "Sure. Thanks, Ms. Stephens."

I was glad she was pleased, but the real test would come thirty seconds from now when I walked into my classroom. My legs felt like lead as I walked down the hall. Would the kids be rolling their eyes, or worse, giving me polite little nods? I felt so exposed. Mom's job was harder than it looked.

I stared at my shoes as I entered Mr. Lambert's algebra class.

"Ah! Here's our Crossroads celebrity in the flesh," Mr. Lambert said from his desk.

I managed a weak smile and settled into my desk.

Paul Pereyo poked me playfully from the seat behind mine. "Awesome job," he said.

A couple of kids nodded, and several were smiling at me. I relaxed a little.

"My mom's a dorky volunteer, too," Casey Lindley said from a couple of rows over. "She makes cupcakes with smiley faces. Barf!"

I chuckled and relaxed my shoulders. They really seemed to have liked it, or at least not totally hated it. I sighed. How was it possible that a few random thoughts in my head the night before had morphed into talking points for the whole school? It was wild . . . a little scary, a little exhilarating, a little . . . *wild*.

"My mom calls people by the wrong names too," Carleigh Brody whispered from the desk in front of mine. "I thought it was just her."

How weird was this? People I barely knew were suddenly talking to me, all because of the Oddcast. I was famous! Well . . . by Crossroads Middle School standards, at least. And fame, I was beginning to realize, wasn't half bad. It wasn't bad at all.

"She said *what?*"

It was drizzly that Saturday, so Mom and I were lazily chilling around the house when Meredith's mom called her around lunchtime. The longer the conversation lasted, the higher Mom's eyebrows rose.

"And it's on the *Internet?*" Mom continued into the phone. "So *anybody* could watch it?"

When she hung up, Mom groaned and buried her face in her hands.

"Talia!" she moaned. "Your first Oddcast commentary was about *me?*"

I grabbed an apple from the kitchen counter, took a bite and patted her shoulder. "Don't worry, Mom," I said as I chewed. "Nobody your age sees the Oddcast."

She peeked at me between splayed fingers. "Except that

it's on the Internet, which limits the potential audience to, oh, about six billion. Are all of your commentaries going to be about me?"

I shrugged. "You have to understand, Mom," I said, taking another bite, "my commentaries aren't really about *you*. They're about Everymom. All my friends can relate. The experiences are universal."

She shook her head and muttered, "I've created a monster."

I shrugged. "You know what's funny? Frankenstein wasn't the name of the monster. It was the name of the doctor who created him."

Mom took a deep breath. "Do I dare see it for myself?" she asked.

She turned on the computer, typed in Crossroads Middle School's Internet address and clicked on the podcast. As I assured her that, no, Peter's name really wasn't Caleb, the color slowly drained from her face.

When the podcast was over, her hands fell into her lap. "How often will you do a commentary?" she asked.

"Weekly."

Mom winced. "But being a dorky volunteer is my only fault, right?" she asked weakly. "I mean, what else could you possibly have to say about me?"

"Well, there's that toenail fungus you've been battling," I said, "and those gray hairs you've started plucking in front of the mirror, and—"

"Talia!" Mom said. "There's such a thing as privacy!"

I tossed my apple into the trash can and put my hands on my hips. "Explain that concept to me, Mom," I said.

"And you better do a good job explaining it, because I have no firsthand experience. What exactly is privacy?"

"Honey, I know I get paid to talk about my family on TV," she said, "but I'm very selective about what I share with my viewers."

"If crayons up the nose makes the cut, what exactly do you consider off-limits?" I challenged.

"Anything you tell me in confidence," she said. "Or anything that could hurt anyone's feelings."

"You've hurt my feelings lots of times," I said with a pout.

Mom's eyes softened. "I know I make you cringe a little now and then, but I've never really hurt your feelings . . . have I?"

I shrugged, then peered at her closely. "I didn't really hurt *your* feelings, did I?"

Mom bit her bottom lip and grinned. "You certainly made me cringe."

I held up the palms of my hands. "Like mother, like daughter."

Mom sighed. "I think," she muttered, "that I've met my match."

I offered her my hand. "A pleasure to meet you, Dr. Frankenstein."

"Talia, E-bay. E-bay, Talia."

E-bay looked suspicious, but he let me shake his paw.

Jake smiled. "Good. You're friends."

E-bay didn't look convinced. "He's growling at me," I said, eyeing Jake's dog nervously.

"No, that's not a growl," Jake assured me.

"I think it's a growl," Mom said, pulling me closer to her side as the three of us crouched in front of E-bay, staring into his chocolate brown eyes.

"E-bay's just a little protective of me," Jake said. "He's a really nice dog. Wouldn't hurt a fly."

I believed Jake; E-bay probably *was* really nice. He just knew we didn't fit in his apartment.

Mom had made our visit to Jake's apartment seem like a spur-of-the-moment decision. We'd been cooped up in the house the whole drizzly Saturday, and I'd assumed we'd be cooped up that whole drizzly Saturday night. But when afternoon turned to evening and I asked Mom what we were having for dinner, she shrugged.

"Hmmm. I hadn't really thought about it." Mom rubbed the back of her neck, then widened her eyes and held up an index finger. "Oh, I have an idea."

"What?" I asked, already feeling suspicious.

"Um, Jake? You remember, Jake, the sportswriter from work? The one we ate pizza with last week? Jake?"

"Yes, Mom. I remember Jake."

"Right. Jake. Anyhow, Jake mentioned that we might want to stop by his apartment this evening . . . just if we were in the neighborhood, or whatever. He said he makes really good pasta and was whipping up a batch tonight."

"You told him we were coming?" I asked, narrowing my eyes.

"No! No, honey, I just said we might stop by, *maybe*, if we didn't have anything else going on."

"Anything else going on?" I repeated slowly. "Like maybe we'd decide at the last minute to throw a neighborhood barbecue or something?"

Mom laughed too loudly. "Oh, Talia, you're such a riot. You know what I mean; you know how we go to Grandma's sometimes, or she and Grandpa come over here, or I thought maybe you'd want to invite Bridget for a sleepover, or . . . I just didn't know if we'd be busy or not."

"But just in case we weren't . . ."

"Right! Just in case we weren't, I told Jake maybe we'd stop by. If we were in the neighborhood."

"And why might we be in Jake's neighborhood?"

Mom flung her hands in the air. "Talia! You're so literal."

I rolled my eyes. "Mom, if you want us to eat at Jake's, why don't you just say so?"

Mom blushed. "I didn't say I want us to eat at Jake's. I just said that *if* we weren't busy, and *if* we were in the neighborhood—"

"Please, Mom. Stop talking in circles. You're making me dizzy." I stared at her for a moment, then nodded slowly. "You really like him, don't you?"

Mom fanned her overheated face with her hand.

"Oh, man. You've got it bad."

So that's how we ended up at Jake's that evening. We just happened to be in the neighborhood.

And now, here I was, standing in front of a growling dog who was wondering why the heck I was there, and frankly, I was wondering the same thing.

Thwack! Jake clapped his hands. "So. My marinara sauce needs just a few more minutes on the stove, then dinner will be ready. Let me finish things up in the kitchen while you two—I don't know—watch TV or something?"

"I've seen enough for one day," Mom said, walking from the foyer over to a couch. She sat at one end, then patted the cushion and motioned for me to sit beside her.

"Talia's doing a weekly commentary for her school's morning broadcast," she said to Jake. "It's uploaded onto the school's Web site as a podcast, so anybody in the whole world, virtually, can watch it if they want."

"Great!" Jake said, walking me over to the couch.

"That's quite an honor, huh? To do a commentary for your school?"

I shrugged and sat beside Mom. "It's no biggie."

"Hey, don't sell yourself short," Jake said, tousling my hair. "You keep it up and you may be your mom's cohost some day."

Mom tossed him a smile. "Or replacement. Go easy on the encouragement. Her commentary was about *me*."

Jake looked quizzical for a moment, then nodded slowly. "Ah. A little tit for tat, huh?"

"She talked about what a dorky volunteer I am at school," Mom said, pinching me playfully.

"No way!" Jake said, smiling broadly and falling back into a well-worn armchair. "Your mom's way too cool to be a dork."

I pinched my lips into a tight smile. "O-*kay*."

"No, really," Jake said, his eyes twinkling. "Your mom is, like, the coolest person I know. I can't imagine her acting dorky."

Mom laughed and put a hand over her face.

"Moms can't be cool," I said. "It's a law of nature."

Jake rubbed his beard, grinning. "So this volunteer work at school: Does she have to wear a name badge and everything?"

I nodded. "And she wears holiday sweaters. You know, pumpkins on Halloween, hearts on Valentine's Day. . . ."

Jake inhaled sharply and grimaced. "*Theme sweaters?* Very uncool."

Now Mom had *both* hands over her face and was giggling so hard, her shoulders shook.

"Okay, you've worn me down," Jake said. He walked over to his desk, grabbed his laptop and plopped back into his chair. "What's the address for your school's Web site? I gotta see this for myself."

"Jake!" Mom moaned.

"Classic!" I said, then told Jake the Web address.

He typed it in, clicked a couple of times to get to the podcast, then watched intently as I gave my commentary. By the end, he was tossing his head back and laughing.

"Does your mom sing in the car when she takes you on field trips?" Jake asked when it was over. By now, E-bay had relaxed and trotted to his side. Jake scratched the dog's neck lazily.

"Yes! And gets the words wrong half the time but keeps singing them anyway."

Jake feigned a look of shock. "Chelsea, I've never seen this side of you before. I have to say, I'm stunned. And frankly, I don't know if I can associate with people who wear holiday theme sweaters and sing the wrong words to songs."

Mom threw a pillow at him, sputtering with laughter. "Stop ganging up on me," she said. "I'll never live down Talia's commentary as it is. How can I ever face Caleb again? Or Peter . . . or whatever that kid's name is."

"You call lots of people by the wrong name," I said, smiling lightly in spite of myself. It was weird to see her flirting, yet she looked so content. I looked closely at Jake. "Are you sure your name is really Jake?"

We all laughed, and E-bay barked in approval of our good moods.

"And we ate pasta, and I played with his dog E-bay, which was pretty cool, and—"

"E-bay?" Bridget asked as we walked toward the Oddcast room Monday morning.

"Yeah. Jake's other dog was named Freeway, so—"

"Never trust a guy who gives his dogs rhyming names," Bridget said.

"Why not?"

Bridget shrugged. "I don't know. On second thought, maybe you can trust him. But never trust people who name their pets after spices."

I tossed a lock of hair off my shoulder. "I think my mom really likes him," I said, quickening my pace so we wouldn't be late. "She was, like, flirting with him. Totally weird."

Bridget and I approached the Oddcast room. Meredith

and Ben were already there, and other staff members were filtering in behind us. Ms. Stephens began handing out scripts.

"Ms. Stephens, can I make an announcement today about a sale at Threads?" asked Meredith. "I know it's not exactly school-related, but tons of girls would be interested—"

"Stick to the script," Bridget said.

Meredith glared at her. "I was asking Ms. Stephens," she said. "And besides, Talia doesn't have to stick to a script. She gets to talk about whatever she wants."

"Not exactly," Ms. Stephens said, adjusting the glasses on her nose. "She has to clear her commentaries with me. And sorry, but a sale at Threads doesn't make the cut."

"Do you own stock or something?" Ben asked, balancing the camcorder on a tripod.

"I'm trying to help make the Oddcast relevant," Meredith said. "I guarantee you that every girl in the school would be interested in knowing about the sale." She cut her eyes at Bridget. "Well, *almost* every girl."

Meredith, Brynne, Carl and I took our seats behind the Oddcast desk.

"I can't even breathe the same oxygen as Bridget without feeling gross," Brynne whispered. "How did we stand her all those years?"

Ms. Stephens cleared her throat from the front of the room. "Guys, let's settle down and do a run-through," she said. "And incidentally, great job on your debut Oddcast Friday. I heard lots of nice feedback. Talia, funny commentary. Did your mom see it?"

I nodded, blushing as all eyes fell on me. "She was a

little freaked out, but she's always told me that writers write what they know . . . and I know what a dorky volunteer Mom is."

The Oddcast staff laughed lightly.

Ms. Stephens raised a single eyebrow. "Right," she said with an easy smile. "But you have a platform now, Talia, and that's a big responsibility. You have to use it wisely. Keep having fun with your commentary, but be mindful of the impact your words might have."

"What's your commentary gonna be about this week?" Ben asked me.

"I'm not sure. Maybe I'll press for improvements at school, like changing rules we don't like."

"Sweet!" Carl said. "I think we should be able to ride skateboards in the halls."

"And take power naps in Mr. Spelman's history class," Ben said as they exchanged high fives.

Ms. Stephens tapped her index fingers together. "Are those the kinds of rules you'd like to challenge, Talia?" she asked.

I twirled a piece of hair. "I dunno. I'd hate to get flattened in the hall by a skateboarder. Power naps, on the other hand, have definite potential."

"Ooooh, pedicures!" Brynne said, raising a hand. "What if there were little booths set up in the cafeteria so we could get our toenails done during lunch?"

"Then your stinky feet would be infringing on my right to enjoy my lunch," Carl said.

Brynne scrunched her nose. "My feet aren't stinky."

Ms. Stephens's strawberry-blond ponytail bounced as she tilted her head. "That's the thing about rules," she said. "They're intended to protect everybody's rights. Once you start monkeying around with them, beware the law of unintended consequences. One person's idea of luxury—lunchtime pedicures—is another person's idea of torture—stinky feet in the cafeteria."

"My feet aren't stinky!" Brynne sputtered, making everybody laugh more.

Bridget made a time-out sign. "Twelve minutes till airtime," she said loudly. "Everybody get in your spot for the run-through."

"*Pssst.*"

I glanced at Meredith, who held a fingertip to her lips. She bent down toward her purse, signaling me to bend down too. She pretended to rustle around in her purse while leaning closer to me.

"I have the petition," she whispered.

"The what?"

"*Ssssshhh!* The petition. To get Bridget fired. I know Ben and Shelley won't sign it, and I don't think I can talk David into it. But with signatures from me, you, Brynne and Carl, we'll have a majority."

"Carl?" I whispered. "Why does Carl want Bridget fired?"

"I told him he could come to my party if he signed it."

I pursed my lips. "Ms. Stephens will never go for it," I said.

"She said we're a team, and if more than half the team wants Bridget gone, what can she say?"

I opened my mouth to respond but sighed with relief as Ms. Stephens quieted the staff to prepare for the Oddcast.

Of *course* I wouldn't sign the petition. But why did I keep finding myself in the middle of this mess?

Meredith caught my eye and mouthed, *"Well?"*

I shrugged. That would have to do for now.

"Payback," Mom told the *Up and At 'Em* audience, "is brutal."

She had taped the show and we were watching it when she got home from work that day.

"I take it you're referring to Talia's following in your footsteps," Chad said.

Mom nodded. "My job makes her feel a little, um, over-exposed periodically."

"No," Chad teased, and the audience laughed.

"Don't feel too sorry for her," Mom said. "She's discovered the perfect revenge. Her school has a closed-circuit TV show—you know, the kids reading announcements, telling ball game scores, recapping spelling bees—that kind of thing. And Talia made the staff."

"How much grief can she cause you by announcing spelling-bee winners?" Chad asked.

"She has her own weekly commentary," Mom said. "She gave her first one on Friday. It's on the school's Web site, so I checked it out over the weekend."

"And?"

"And it was kinda about me." She cringed.

"A little tit for tat, huh?" Chad asked.

"Something like that. But who could imagine she'd have anything embarrassing to say about *me?*"

Chad mugged for the audience and they chuckled.

"Her debut commentary explored my shortcomings as a school volunteer," Mom said. "I thought I was a great volunteer—perky, cheerful, the whole bit. Give me a can of shortening, sugar and some food coloring and I can whip up a classroom treat for any and all occasions. I even made little trees for Arbor Day one year and used tiny squiggles of licorice to simulate George Washington's dour expression for Presidents' Day cookies." Mom stretched her lips to ape the expression. "But apparently, these are the very qualities that doomed me to doofusness."

"You do get a little carried away over the holidays," Chad said. "We've all seen your theme sweaters."

"I should've anticipated this development, just as I should have anticipated the day Talia would beat me at tennis," Mom said. "It's all part of the natural order: parents teaching their kids how to make their way in the world, then having their kids rub it in their faces by doing it better than their parents ever dreamed of."

120

"Just tell me you're unloading the theme sweaters at a yard sale," Chad said.

"I like my theme sweaters," Mom said, pouting. "And no matter what Talia says, I still say my George Washington cookies are delicious. And that's the truth."

Mom turned off the TV and tugged my ponytail. "I guess I don't get the last word anymore, huh?" she said.

21

"If you could name the school after a fruit, which one would you pick and why?"

Most kids were giving us blank stares or rolling their eyes, but a few were hammy enough to mug for the camera and give an answer.

"Prune School, 'cause we're the pits," a chubby boy responded, shaking a victory fist into the camera.

"Aren't you the clever one," Bridget said.

She, Shelley and Ben had invited me to come along during lunch period to interview kids in the hall for an upcoming Oddcast segment.

We inched farther down the hall, Ben trailing us with the camcorder. "If you could name the school after a fruit, which one would you pick and why?" Bridget asked the next person who walked by.

"Um, a peach, 'cause we're peachy?" a freckle-faced girl responded shyly.

"An orange, 'cause we have appeal!" her friend volunteered, and they high-fived each other.

"Yup. A bunch of real geniuses at this school," Bridget said.

"In which case we'd name ourselves the Banana School, right?" Shelley quipped. "Bunch? Banana?"

"Gee, I don't get it," Bridget deadpanned.

It had been a weird week. Bridget and I had patched things up, but she was spending every spare minute on the Oddcast, so unless I tagged along, we weren't hanging out much. Mer and Brynne kept bugging me about their petition, and that stupid party was coming up. . . .

Mom was disappearing into her bedroom for at least half an hour every evening after dinner to "wash her hair" (talk to Jake on the phone), so she wasn't offering much help in sorting out my feelings.

Thank heaven I had my commentary to concentrate on. It was due Thursday, and I was getting more comfortable spilling my thoughts on paper. I worked on it every night after homework, typing a few lines, deleting some, adding some more, and sometimes just trashing it and starting all over again. Most people's idea of misery, I know, but I really loved it. I could hear a kind of melody in my head if my words were flowing, and it was the best feeling in the world. By Wednesday night, I was ready to hit Save. Ms. Stephens would still have to approve it, of course, but writing felt so *right*. I couldn't wait till Friday.

● ● ●

"Reporting live from Crossroads Middle School, this is Talia Farrow with 'Talia Talk.' "

Okay, maybe I *was* still a little nervous. My stomach had decided to dance the rumba just as Ben tilted the camcorder toward me for our Friday-morning Oddcast.

"Some people have told me I should use my commentary to try to change school rules that nobody likes," I said into the camera, smoothing the trendy peasant shirt Meredith had instructed me to wear. She'd even talked me into putting a little blush on my cheeks. She'd declared me camera-ready when I got to school.

"I'm pretty sure that nobody likes homework and everybody likes chewing gum," I continued, following Bridget's cue to slow my pace. "Most kids hate the dress code, and a lot of them think we need more time to change classes. (Note to future business tycoons: Invent a locker combination that's easy to use! Your billions, and the gratitude of kids everywhere, are awaiting you.)

"Now, I don't know that I can single-handedly transform Crossroads Middle School into a homework-free, gum-chewing paradise, but I do have a few ideas about what could truly make our school a better place. So if I ruled the school, here's what I would do:

"Change the name *middle school* to *fabulous school*. Nobody likes being in the middle of anything. Everyone likes being fabulous.

"Forbid students to wear pants that make a swishy sound when they change classes. Corduroy comes to mind. I hate that sound.

"Forbid the nutrition police (you know you who are) to tell us how many fat grams and preservatives are in our food when we're trying to eat our chicken nuggets.

"Forbid cool kids to roll their eyes at the rest of us. We may be uncool, but you're rude.

"Forbid teachers to have teachers' pets. (Oh, yes you do, and we all know it!)

"Require teachers to play music during tests. It soothes the savage breast, remember? Of course, everybody has different tastes, so we'll need to appoint a music deputy to select the tunes. I nominate myself.

"Require teachers to provide tasty snacks during class. Who can think when their blood sugar is low?

"Eliminate alphabet discrimination! Require teachers to call the roll backward. The Zacharys of the world are tired of their inferiority complex.

"How's that for a start? I don't claim to have all the answers, but I think my rules would make fabulous school a more fabulous place. Since these rules are such no-brainers, I'll assume the principal will approve them right away. So if you'll excuse me, I'd better get started on my music selections.

"Signing off for now, this is Talia Farrow for the Crossroads Oddcast."

22

"Hey, Talia! Liked the Oddcast yesterday."

"Thanks."

I fingered my necklace with one hand, clutching Meredith's present with the other as I inched my way along the outskirts of the crowded dance floor. The strobe lights were already pulsing and the deejay cranking up the music by the time I got to the party. I glanced from one face to the next, trying not to make eye contact. A few people were dancing, but most of them were like me: hugging the walls like novice ice skaters who didn't want to venture too far from the safety bar.

I'd felt out of place since I walked inside. Everybody was wearing blue jeans except me. I was wearing a stupid dress. Mom had insisted. ("It's a dance, honey!" *Grrrrr* . . .) I knew most of the kids at the party, but for some reason, they looked like strangers under the strobe lights. Carl, the guy from the Oddcast who'd signed the petition to nail an invite (whoopee!) looked like a Martian with the neon lights casting shades of orange, pink and purple on his face. Mark was just Mark at school, but here, he looked right through me like I was invisible, even when I smiled and told him his hair looked nice. Creepy.

I bit my fingernails.

"Hi, Talia."

I turned toward the voice. "Meredith . . . hi. Happy birthday."

"The gift table is that way," Meredith said, pointing across the room while eyeing the wrapped box in my hand. "Threads?"

"What? Oh . . . yeah."

Meredith's mom stepped up behind her. "Meredith!" she snapped. "Don't you dare ask your guests where their gifts came from! Can't you simply say thank you?"

Meredith rolled her eyes. "Thank you," she said to me, exaggerating the words like I was deaf.

"I'll take that, Talia, dear," her mom said, taking the gift from me. "We're so glad you could come. And you look darling! Love the dress. Just make yourself at home. Mingle, or grab a snack. Or dance! Do you like to dance?"

"Um . . ."

"Mark, why don't you dance with Talia?"

Oh no. Meredith's mom grabbed Mark Miller's arm and pulled him toward me. He looked like he was waiting for a firing squad to aim their guns.

"That's okay," I said quickly, pulling my hair behind my ear. "I'm not really much of a dancer."

"Nonsense!" Meredith's mom said. "Mark, give her a spin around the dance floor." She gave both of us a little shove. We exchanged sideways glances and Mark shoved his hands in his pockets.

"Uh . . . ," he said, then shifted his weight from side to side. I halfheartedly snapped my fingers to the beat and bobbed my head a little. Mark gazed at his feet and I stared at the gift table, where Meredith's mom was balancing my present on the pile and giving me a thumbs-up.

Yuck. Why had I come to this party? And why was I self-conscious in front of Mark Miller, the kid whose nervous stomach had kept the custodian trudging to our classroom with a mop and bucket at least once a week all through elementary school? He was three inches shorter than me and dancing like somebody was throwing lit matches at his feet. What a dork! Why in the world was I nervous around *him*?

Because I was even dorkier, shifting my weight and snapping my fingers in the stupid dress I'd worn in my piano recital, the one where I'd barfed on my teacher's shoes. If Bridget had been here, she'd be howling at my stiff little dance moves. *Turn hips now*, I was instructing myself. *Bend elbows now. Point thumb in random direction now.* It felt as natural as doing a polka on top of a telephone pole. How many people were looking at me? Certainly not Mark, who was still staring at his shoes.

We both acted like we'd won the lottery when the music finally wound down. We clapped our hands half-heartedly, then slunk off to separate corners of the room.

128

Brynne walked up to me, swaying to the beat of the music and eyeing me up and down. "Nice dress."

I blushed.

"Where's Bridget tonight?" she asked. "Off taking graduate courses at nerd academy?"

"What? Oh, I don't know where she is."

"I can't figure you out, Talia. One day, you're hanging out with us in the cafeteria, and the next, you're back with Barfy Bridget."

I scanned the dance floor, just to avoid looking at Brynne. "Didn't realize I was in such hot demand," I said testily.

Brynne huffed. "You know, sometimes you seem totally cool, and sometimes you try to act like you're better than everybody else."

My eyebrows arched. "Like *I'm* better? Are you serious? I'm the dork standing here in a dress!"

"Exactly!" Brynne sniffed. "The only advice I can give to you is lose the attitude. Oh, and lose Bridget! Have you signed the petition yet?"

I shrugged. *Good move, Talia,* I thought. *Just keep shrugging. Never take a stand, and everybody will like you. Right? RIGHT?*

Man, I hated myself right now.

"Love the dress." I looked up and saw Meredith walking toward us, curling her lip. "And thanks for keeping Mark occupied on the dance floor. I only invited him because our mothers are friends. Dweeb."

"I was just telling Talia that Bridget is, like, totally weighing her down," Brynne said.

Meredith nodded sharply. "It's way past time to move on, Talia," she said.

"I guess she *can* be a little over the top," I murmured.

" 'Over the top'?" Meredith said. "She's a loon."

"Funny that you say that. Her middle name is Luna, you know. She hates it."

Meredith and Brynne dropped their jaws, sputtered in laughter and exchanged high fives. "Luna!" Meredith squealed, prompting Brynne to laugh even harder.

I smiled halfheartedly, but my heart sank.

I sneaked a peek at my watch. I'd endured this agony for approximately thirteen minutes, and Mom wasn't scheduled to pick me up for another two hours and seventeen minutes. I managed to toss a quick smile at Brynne and Meredith, then ducked out into a hallway and called Mom on my cell phone, pressing the keys like they were eject buttons on a doomed spaceship.

"Hello?" Mom answered in a tinkly voice after a couple of rings.

"Mom, can you come get me?" I asked, the words rushing out.

"Talia? Honey, is something wrong?"

I pressed my finger against my lip. "No. I just want to go home."

"Um, honey, actually, I'm having dinner with Jake right now. We just ordered. Do you think you could hang in there for another hour or so?"

My lips tightened. "You didn't tell me you were having dinner with Jake."

"I didn't think it mattered, since you'd be at the party anyway."

I shook my head but didn't say anything.

"Talia, we can come now if you absolutely need us to," Mom said.

"We"? Who said anything about "we"? I just needed my mom. Why wasn't she curled up with an afghan in her pajamas watching a chick flick on television? That was what my mom did on Saturday nights. Or that was what she *used* to do. Now here I was, stuck at this awful party, listening to her use pronouns like *we*.

"It's okay," I muttered. "Enjoy your dinner."

"Are you sure, honey?"

"I'm sure. Just get here as soon as you can after you're through at the restaurant. Please?"

"Okay, sweetie. Try to have a good time, okay?"

"Please just hurry."

• • •

Forty minutes. Forty-five minutes. An hour. An hour and twelve minutes. An hour and sixteen minutes.

Where was Mom?

I kept glancing out the window, checking to see if she was here yet. Since when did it take an hour and sixteen minutes to eat dinner?

Make that an hour and twenty-four minutes. *Where was she?*

I'd given up trying to make small talk or flap around on

the dance floor. (Not that anyone was asking me.) Instead, I stood close to the snack table and mindlessly munched cheese curls. Every once in a while, someone would walk up and say hi to me. "Hi," I responded. Whatever. Frankly, *nobody* seemed to be having a very good time at this party.

Thank heaven Meredith finally started opening presents. That would kill a good half hour or so. She oohed and aahed over her Threads gifts, acting shocked—shocked!—that everyone seemed to know exactly what to give her.

"Thank heaven for gift registries," I overheard Meredith's mom telling another adult. "Otherwise, we'd be at the mall all day tomorrow making returns."

"Oh, this will go super with my eyes!" Meredith cooed, holding a stretchy blue shirt against her face. *Gag.*

One hour thirty-six minutes.

"Ooooh, Kayla!" Meredith said, holding up a belt. "The belt I've been dying to have! How did you *know?*"

Puh-leeze. *Where was Mom?*

"Cute earrings," Meredith said with a sour expression as she opened the next present. "Um, they're not from Threads, right?" she asked Mark, who blushed and stared at his shoes.

"Meredith!" her mom snapped.

"They're fine, they're fine!" Meredith said. "I was checking to see where they're from in case I need to . . . whatever. They're fine. Thanks, Mark."

Poor Mark, I thought with a snicker. *Don't you know you have to follow the rules?*

"Cute sweater, Talia," Meredith said as she opened the gift that Mom had dutifully selected from her registry. "Purple is, like, my signature color. You must be psychic!"

Grrrrrrr . . . One hour forty-three minutes and one-half. *WHERE WAS MOM?*

Aaaaahhhh . . . hallelujah! I saw the glare of headlights through the window and peered closely. Drat! Not Mom's car. But then my cell phone rang.

"Honey? It's Mom. We're right outside."

I peered closer out into the parking lot.

"I don't see your car."

"We're in Jake's."

Well, of course you are.

I grabbed my purse, slung it over my shoulder and made the obligatory trek to Meredith's mom. "I've got to go now; my mom's here," I said. "Thanks so much for having me."

"You have to leave so soon?" she asked.

I smiled apologetically. "Yeah, but I had a really good time."

"We certainly enjoyed having you. Thank you so much for coming. Hold on just a second and I'll have Meredith come over and tell you—"

"Uh, I really have to go. Sorry. Mom's in some big hurry."

I practically ran out the door, then through the parking lot to Jake's car. I got in the backseat and slammed the door shut.

"Killer party, huh?" Jake asked.

I slunk lower into my seat.

"What was so awful about it?" Mom asked, turning to face me.

I cracked a window and held my face closer.

"Talia?" Mom said. "Are you giving us the silent treatment?"

"It was just a stupid party, okay?" I said.

Silence.

"Talia, why are you in such a terrible mood?" Mom asked, craning her neck again to see me.

More silence.

"I guess the party wasn't such a good idea after all?" Mom said. I made some noncommittal grunt from the back of my throat.

Jake turned on his radio and started whistling along. Mom stared straight ahead. A few minutes passed, and Jake finally turned into our neighborhood.

"Hey," he said cheerily, "I've got an idea. Can I challenge you girls to a game of Scrabble?"

Hot tears suddenly filled my eyes. "I don't think so," I said, my voice trembling.

Jake turned into our driveway. Mom murmured apologies to him while she hustled me out of the car. She closed the front door behind us as soon as we were in the house.

"Talia," she said, "what is going on?"

Tears spilled onto my cheeks. At first, I brushed them away angrily with my fist, but they kept coming, so I just let them flow as Mom guided me toward the couch.

"What happened?" she asked, sitting beside me on the couch and stroking my hair.

"Nothing," I whimpered. "It was just a stupid party. I hated it. Everybody there was acting so snotty and fake. Meredith's mom made me dance with stupid Mark Miller, and I looked like a total moron. Then Meredith and Brynne started telling me how Bridget and I are, like, the biggest losers in school, and . . ."

A sob churned up my throat and drowned out my words. Mom pulled me into her arms.

"Then," I continued through my tears, "I called you and you hadn't even told me you were going out with Jake tonight. . . ."

"But, honey—"

"And I told you I was having a horrible time and wanted to go home, and you said you'd come as soon as you finished dinner, and, like, an hour and forty minutes later . . ."

"But, Talia, we were—"

"And then I'm in the car with Jake, feeling totally crummy and not wanting to talk, knowing I'm making you mad by acting like a brat, and feeling totally guilty because you're finally interested in a nice guy and I'm just ruining the whole thing, but I can't help it because I'm feeling like I'm going to cry and I don't know what to say, and then . . . Scrabble! Mom, I'm sorry. I know you like Jake, and I like him, too, but *Scrabble*! It's like . . . *Dad's* thing."

I buried my head in Mom's chest and cried some more as she ran her fingers through the back of my hair. We sat there for a long time before I realized Mom was dabbing her eyes too. Then I rubbed *her* hair. Eventually, we fell asleep right there on the couch, tasting each other's salty tears and tangled in each other's arms.

"Bridge! Thank heaven you're home. Can you come over?"

Silence.

"Bridget?"

More silence.

I held my cell phone closer to my mouth and adjusted my position on my bed. "Hello? Hello?"

"I'm here," Bridget finally said, softly.

"Bridge, I have to tell you about my horrible night. Mom made her Sunday roast beef. Come eat with us and let me spill my guts."

Silence.

"Hello?"

"Sorry. I can't make it."

"What? Why not?"

Pause. "I already heard about your night."

My stomach tightened. "What do you mean?"

"I thought you weren't going to Meredith's party," Bridget said in a small but steely voice.

I hadn't actually told her that . . . had I? "I *wish* I hadn't gone," I said quickly, trying to push past the awkwardness. "It was awful." I paused. "Who told you I went?"

Silence.

"Bridget! What's up with the silent treatment?"

I heard her sniffling on the other end of the phone.

"Bridge? Golden Gate Bridget? Are you crying?"

She sniffled some more. "I don't know why it takes me so long to catch on. You've been trying to dump me since school started," she said, her voice cracking. "I guess I'm just slow, huh?"

My hand clenched the phone tighter. "What are you talking about?"

"You don't have to tell me about Meredith's party, Talia," Bridget said, her voice stronger now. "Meredith already did. She called to rub it in."

I tightened my lips. "What did she say?"

"Uh . . . where to start. . . . I guess we could start with you blabbing my middle name to the Snob Squad."

"Wha—? Oh! Bridget! I didn't mean to."

"Right. Was that before or after you signed the petition to get me fired?"

"I never signed that petition!" I said, leaping from my bed.

Pause. Bridget was crying again. My heart sank. I could bear just about anything but making Bridget cry.

"Bridget, I never signed that stupid petition! I swear!"

"Why didn't you tell me about it?" she asked, her voice shaking through anger and tears.

I felt like I'd been kicked in the stomach. At that moment, I would have shaved my head to make Bridget stop crying.

"You're right. I should have told you. I'm sorry. But, Bridget, you're totally misunderstanding. I hated Meredith's party. And I wasn't dissing you. I was too busy standing there in my stupid piano-recital dress thinking about what a total zero I was, about how I didn't belong. And then my mom was late picking me up because she and Jake . . . well, it's a long story, but the only thing I wanted to do was to talk to you."

Bridget sniffled. "In the immortal words of Mick Jagger, you can't always get what you want." I heard her blowing into a tissue. "I get it, Talia, with you trying to figure out what kind of friends you want to have. But you might give a little more thought to what kind of friend you want to *be*."

I grappled for words, but none came to mind.

"Talia, I don't mean to sound snotty," Bridget said softly, "but I gotta go. See you around."

"Pssssst."

I ignored Meredith.

"Pssssst!"

I stared straight ahead.

"PSSSSST!"

I jerked my head in Meredith's direction. *"What?"*

"God! You don't have to bite my head off. Are you going to sign the petition already? With you, me, Brynne and Carl, we'll have a majority. If we turn it in today, maybe we can get rid of Bridget by tomorrow."

The last thing I wanted was to face Meredith in the Oddcast office that morning, but I had no choice. I'd tried apologizing again to Bridget when I walked in, but she'd turned her back to me and started talking to Ben. So here I was, stuck behind the Oddcast desk with the Snob Squad, who had ruined my only real friendship.

"I'm not signing your stupid petition!" As miserable as I was, I couldn't help noting that this answer felt much better than a shrug.

Meredith scowled, then gave Brynne an "I told you so" look.

"*Awwww*," Brynne mocked. "Are Bridget's feelings hurt because she didn't get invited to Mer's party? Well, tell her to grow up. Mer can't invite the whole school, can she?"

I spun to face Meredith, my face hot with rage. "Why did you tell Bridget I was making fun of her?"

Her jaw dropped dramatically. "As if!"

"Like we don't have anything better to talk about than you and Loser Bridget Luna," Brynne said with a sneer.

"God," Meredith said. "I wish I hadn't invited *you* to my party, either."

That *so* made two of us.

"Hey, Talia," Shelley called from across the room, "funny commentary Friday. What are you going to talk about this week?"

I took a deep breath. "Um, I don't really know yet," I said.

Except now I did.

"She hates me," I said, wiping away a tear with the tissue Mom handed me.

"Oh, honey." Mom squeezed me closer to her on the couch and kissed my cheek.

"The worst part is that Bridget was right," I said, blowing my nose into the tissue as Mom plucked a fresh one from the box. "I was, like, friend shopping."

"No, you weren't, sweetie. All you did was accept an invitation to a party."

"If it was so innocent, why didn't I tell Bridget about it? I lied to her, Mom. I had the best friend in the world, and I tossed her aside like . . . like . . . like this tissue." I let the soggy tissue drop from my fingertips. "Bridget's right to hate me. I'm hate-worthy."

I buried my face in Mom's chest and cried harder. Mom

patted me for a minute, then gently pulled me back so she could look me in the eye.

"Let's call her," she said. "Let's take her out for ice cream and get this straightened out."

I shook my head. "I don't think ice cream can fix this problem. Besides, she wouldn't go. She wouldn't even sit with me in the lunchroom today. Why would she want to hang around somebody who lies to her and gossips behind her back?"

"You gossiped?" Mom asked anxiously.

I nodded as my face crumpled into another sob. "Meredith and Brynne are always talking about how obnoxious Bridget is, and every once in a while, I kinda agree with them . . . or at least make them think I'm agreeing with them by not defending her. I told them at Meredith's party that Bridget was 'over the top,' or something stupid like that. And I told them Bridget's middle name, which she totally hates. They wasted no time blabbing it to her."

Mom hugged me for a minute, smoothing my hair. "Honey, everybody makes mistakes," she said quietly. "The test of true character is how people handle their mistakes."

I tightened my lips. "I've already decided how I'm going to handle mine," I said. I gave Mom a wobbly smile and stood up. "Thanks for talking to me, Mom."

I walked to my bedroom. Time to write.

• • •

Talia Talk: I'm Over It
    You know what I hate? Phonies. Fakes. Gossips. People with gift registries for stupid birthday parties.

I hate that somebody can like you in elementary school and hate you in middle school because suddenly you aren't cool anymore. Whatever *cool* means. I hate what people in our school consider cool: the right clothes, the right jewelry, the right look. I hate that people in our school don't need any truly valuable qualities—intelligence, compassion, a sense of humor—as long as they have a ceramic hair straightener.

I hate people who talk about other people behind their backs, or even say snotty things to their faces if they think they can get away with it. I hate that people who treat other people like dirt seem to have loads of friends.

But most of all, I hate that sometimes I act like the people I hate. I'm not sure why I do it. Am I trying to fit in? To be more popular? To be polite, so other people won't think I'm looking down on them for acting snotty? Maybe I do it just because it's easier: go along to get along.

Except that I don't want to get along anymore. It's one thing to hate other people; it's another to hate myself. Right now, I hate myself. And I hate it when that happens. So will I get invited to fewer parties, or have fewer "friends," or have to concern myself with fewer gift registries? I don't care. I'm over it.

● ● ●

"Talia, can I talk to you for a minute?"

I glanced up from my seat in the cafeteria and saw Ms. Stephens standing there, holding my commentary.

"Sure," I said. "Take your pick," I said, motioning toward the empty chairs at my table.

I surveyed the cafeteria as she sat down, watching other kids giggle, nudge each other, grab each other's fries. Bridget was sitting with Shelley and Ben; I'd tried to catch her eye several times, but it never happened.

Ms. Stephens cleared her throat as she settled into a chair. "I'll cut to the chase," she said, putting the commentary on the table. "You can't read this on the Oddcast."

I stabbed a lettuce leaf absently with my fork. "Why not?"

"Many reasons come to mind, but it's always a red flag when a writer uses the word *hate* seventeen times in a single commentary."

"You counted?"

She smiled warmly. "Not really. But I got the idea."

I stabbed more lettuce with my fork. "I was just being honest." I glanced at her, then stared back down at my salad.

"Honesty's good, Talia, but you'll be going to this school for three years. You can't alienate yourself from people."

"I don't care. Everybody hates me anyway."

Ms. Stephens shook her head impatiently. "Talia, I don't know what happened, but you're burning too many bridges with this essay. And whoever these people are that you supposedly 'hate' . . . well, they have feelings too, you know."

I looked at her evenly. "You obviously don't know these people very well."

Ms. Stephens rested her elbows on the table and leaned toward me. "Sure I do. I was eleven once too. There were plenty of parties I wasn't invited to, and plenty I wish I hadn't been. You guys didn't invent cliques, or gossip, or catty remarks. And you made the point yourself that things like this are never black and white. There are lots of gray areas."

I was silent for a moment, then felt my eyes fill with tears that I quickly blinked back. "Meredith and Brynne ratted me out, and now Bridget hates me," I said, my words tumbling out like dominoes as my voice cracked.

Ms. Stephens's eyes softened. She touched my hand. "You probably aren't as mad at them as you are at yourself."

"True. But I hate them, too. And I miss Bridget."

"*Hmmmm,*" Ms. Stephens said, tapping her index finger on my essay. "This commentary tells me what you hate. Wouldn't it be more instructive to write about what you *don't* hate? What you believe in?"

"I don't know what I believe in," I said.

"Sure you do. You know better now than you did last week. That's the great thing about crummy experiences."

I thought for a few moments.

"I know that real friends, even if they aren't perfect, beat fake friends who think they're perfect," I finally said.

I thought some more. "I know real friendship has nothing to do with popularity," I continued. "I know real friends make you feel good about yourself, not horrible. I know real friendship stands the test of time and doesn't end when somebody cooler comes along."

Ms. Stephens cupped her chin in her hand. "Sounds like you have a lot to write about."

My lips squeezed into a smile. "I'll take another crack at it," I said.

She nodded. "Good idea." She sighed. "I'm starving. Mind if I join you for lunch?"

26

Mom kept the engine idling while I ran up Bridget's driveway and rang her doorbell.

Her mom answered the door.

"Hi, Mrs. Scott," I said softly. "Is Bridget home?"

Bridget's mom tugged lightly on her ear. "She's not, honey. She's at Shelley's right now."

"Oh." I fingered my essay nervously.

"I think they're working on the Oddcast," Mrs. Scott said. "I can call her on her cell phone if it's an emergency. . . ."

"No, no. I just wanted to drop something off."

Mrs. Scott craned her neck and waved at Mom in the car, mouthing a hello. Mom waved back.

"So how's the romance going?" Bridget's mom asked, giving me a conspiratorial grin.

The *what?* Oh . . . Actually, now that I thought of it, I realized I hadn't seen Jake since Saturday night.

"Fine, I guess."

"Maybe your mom and I can go out to lunch one day soon . . . you know, get caught up."

"Sure. She'd like that." I cleared my throat and handed Mrs. Scott the essay. "So . . . you'll give this to Bridget?"

She nodded. "And I'll have her call you."

"That's okay," I said too quickly. "I mean, it's fine if she wants to, but she doesn't have to."

Her mom winked at me. "She'll call you."

● ● ●

I was already seated when Bridget walked into the cafeteria the next day.

I sucked in my breath. It was Thursday, four days since she'd spoken to me, and despite her mom's promise, she hadn't called me after I'd dropped off the commentary the afternoon before. She had ignored me during the Oddcast that morning, except for a few snippy instructions. Did she hate my commentary? Did she still hate *me?* Would she *always* hate me?

I didn't have the nerve to face her as I picked at my food in the cafeteria, once again sitting by myself. I saw Shelley waving to her from the corner of my eye.

Time dragged by. I sighed, then glumly opened a textbook to study. If I was going to be friendless, I could at least aim for friendless and smart.

As my eyes glazed vacantly at this week's vocabulary

words—*indelible, indigenous, indignant*—I heard a clink, then saw a pen rolling toward me on the floor from behind. I leaned down to pick it up, then saw Bridget's eyes lock with mine.

"Dropped my pen," she said.

I put it in her hand, holding her gaze. "I'm really, *really* sorry." It was all I could say.

"Yeah, well, I kinda dropped my pen on purpose. Your commentary was pretty spectabulous."

A smile flooded my face. Bridget responded by sucking in her cheeks and widening her eyes for her classic piranha imitation. We burst into laughter.

"Come sit with Shelley and me," Bridget said, still grudgingly, but with twinkly eyes. As I stood up, our heads bumped together, making us laugh even harder. Laughing with Bridget. It was the best feeling in the whole world.

● ● ●

"Reporting live from Crossroads Middle School, this is Talia Farrow with 'Talia Talk.' "

I cleared my throat and read on, looking into the camcorder and ignoring Mer's eyes boring into me from her Oddcast seat.

"A confession: I didn't want to do a commentary for the Oddcast.

"At least, I didn't *think* I did.

"I guess my best friend knew better, because she talked me into it.

"My mom is on a local TV show, and I thought the last

thing I wanted to do was follow in her footsteps. There's nothing like having a spotlight shone on your goofiest, most embarrassing moments to make you want to sign up for the Witness Protection Program. I've been so overexposed that I feel like handing out shades as a public service so people won't be blinded by the glare when they look at me. A commentary of my own? I'd rather have my tonsils yanked out.

"So when my BFF practically dragged me over to meet Ms. Stephens on the first day of school to tell her what a great Oddcaster I'd be, I felt like a lobster selected from a tank for somebody's dinner. With friends like those . . . well, you know the rest.

"Why am I telling you this now? Because my BFF was right. I really do love writing, and even though I've only been at it a few weeks now, I've had a blast so far with 'Talia Talk.'

"Since my BFF was being a good friend to me without me even realizing it, it got me thinking about whether what I *think* I want in a friend is what I *really* want in a friend. I think I know better now than I did last week what I really want. A good friend knows you better than you know yourself sometimes. A good friend gives you a little shove now and then (or, okay, a full-fledged dropkick) to push you past your comfort zone. A good friend helps you be brave, but loves you even if you chicken out. A good friend makes you laugh at anything and everything—including yourself.

"It wasn't hard to come up with this list. All I had to do was think of my BFF. Harder was coming up with my next list. Once I knew what kind of friend I want to *have*, it was time to decide what kind of friend I want to *be*. After some trial and error, here's what I've decided: I want to be a friend who is loyal. If I have something to grouse about, I'll grouse *to* my friend, not *about* her.

"I want to be a friend who is honest. Saying what's on your mind—(as long as it's not snarky)—should make you closer to your BFF. If it doesn't, maybe you have the wrong friend.

"I want to be a friend who is trustworthy. No lies allowed, not even mini-lies like fibs. A mini-lie is a maxi-betrayal.

"I want to be a friend who is flexible. Good friendships bend in strong winds; shallow friendships snap like twigs. BFFs stand the test of time.

"I want to be a friend who is dependable. When my BFF needs me, I want to be there for her.

"It's funny . . . everything I want to *be* as a friend is everything I already *have* in a friend.

"And I'll never take that for granted again.

"Signing off for now, this is Talia Farrow for the Crossroads Oddcast."

Bridget smiled. "Cut."

27

"Bombs away!"

Shelley and I exchanged smiles and braced for the impact, knowing Bridget was about to charge us from behind.

"Ker-PLOW!"

Bridget skated into our interlocked hands, knocking them loose, grabbing one of Shelley's and one of mine.

Shelley wobbled for a minute before regaining her balance. "Bridget!" she moaned. "You know I'm a lousy skater."

"The skating rink is no place for sissies," Bridget reasoned.

"I should've worn a crash helmet," Shelley said.

The three of us skated hand in hand, gliding in unison and singing along to the song blaring over the loudspeakers.

"Why'd you have to go and make things so complicated?" Bridget sang exuberantly, raising our hands skyward. Shelley

wobbled again. Her left knee buckled as her right leg splayed out in front of her.

Plunk. She was down.

"Officers, we have a man down eastbound on Skate-a-way Boulevard," Bridget monotoned, pretending to talk into a walkie-talkie. "Victim is responsive but shows no signs of basic coordination. Recommend we suspend her skating permit indefinitely."

"Ow!" Shelley wailed as Bridget and I each grabbed a hand and helped her to her feet. But as soon as she was vertical again, a freckle-faced little kid came barreling into the back of her knees.

"Wha . . . whoa!" Shelley screamed, spinning her arms like propellers as the clueless freckle-faced kid plowed ahead without looking back.

Plunk. She was down again.

"Shelley, you don't need a crash helmet," I said, helping her up again. "You need body armor."

"What I need," Shelley groused while dusting off the back of her pants, "is a break." She nodded toward the concession stand.

"I'm not sure we can trust you with refreshments," Bridget deadpanned. "You have to coordinate the tongue, jaw and throat muscles. It's pretty tricky."

"It's okay; I'm really good with my tongue muscle," Shelley said, sticking her tongue out at Bridget.

We laughed and followed her off the rink. Our skates clunked on the thin, faded carpet of the concession area. We ordered Cokes and French fries, then sat at a plastic table.

"I'm glad you two are friends again," Shelley said, nibbling a wilted fry. "It was exhausting listening to Bridget tell me how evil you were."

"Being evil isn't everything it's cracked up to be," I hissed, scrunching up my face menacingly and making claws of my hands.

We giggled and slurped from our straws.

"Seriously, your commentary was really nice," Shelley said. "Everybody was talking about it on the school bus."

I raised an eyebrow. "Everybody?"

Shelley giggled and nodded. "Yeah. Meredith was fuming, telling her friends that she'd tried to reach out to you and you just weren't ready to be helped."

"*Awwww*," Bridget said. "She's too kind for her own good."

"Then she got all snotty and said she didn't even like the sweater you gave her for her birthday," Shelley continued.

I dropped my jaw in mock horror. "Didn't like the sweater! Oooh, how can I ever make it up to her?"

We laughed and munched on more greasy fries. "Didn't you get her something off her registry?" Shelley said.

"Of course I did. Those were the rules." We laughed lightly. "But I guess a girl's entitled to change her mind."

"I heard she's crushing on Chase Stewart," Shelley said. "Were they dancing together at her party?"

I tossed a hand in the air. "Like I would have noticed. I was too busy speed-dialing my mom's cell phone. And then, my mom was like *two hours late* picking me up. . . ."

I huffed at the memory.

"So how's it going with her and Jakey?" Bridget asked, curling her lips into a gooey-sweet smile.

I shrugged. "I haven't seen him since they picked me up from Meredith's party. I was kinda awful to him."

"What did you do?" Shelley asked, leaning in closer.

"I didn't really do anything. . . . It's just . . . he was trying to make small talk—he's really funny—and I was kinda quiet and bratty, you know? I feel bad. He's a nice guy."

"Why don't you get him a gift to make it up to him?" Bridget said. "Maybe something off Meredith's registry? I hear she has exquisite taste."

We laughed, but I felt a little stab in my stomach. "He might be at the house now," I said. "Mom probably cooked him dinner or something . . . although, come to think of it, I haven't heard her talking to him on the phone in a few days." I shrugged. "But he's probably there. I'll be extra nice when I see him."

"Kaia Jacobs's mom is dating a guy who owns a jewelry store," Shelley said conspiratorially. "That's why she's got such cute earrings all the time. I could see some definite advantages to having a mom who dates."

"Mrs. Farrow's boyfriend is a sportscaster," Bridget said. "Unless Talia has to write an essay about Tiger Woods, there's probably not much in it for her."

I knew she was teasing, but my stomach felt even heavier. I fingered my straw nervously. "I just want my mom to be happy. . . ."

"Wow. Deep," Shelley said.

I blushed. "Not deep. Just true. Mom really lights up around Jake, you know? I've never seen that side of her before. Well, maybe when my dad was still alive, but I don't remember that very well."

"My mom lights up around butter-pecan ice cream," Shelley said.

I propped my elbow on the table and slumped forward, dropping my chin in my hand. "I like it when my mom lights up," I said.

It was like Ms. Stephens had said: crummy experiences help you know what you believe in.

I popped the last fry from my box into my mouth. "Mmmmmm," I said. "Greasy French fries are way underrated."

● ● ●

Mom was already in her pajamas when Mrs. Scott dropped me off from the skating rink.

"I made popcorn," she said, kissing my cheek as I walked in the front door. "You pick the movie." Mom nodded toward the DVDs piled on a bookshelf next to our TV.

I glanced anxiously around the room. "Just the two of us?"

Mom's eyebrows knitted together. "I invited Brad Pitt, but he couldn't make it."

She pinched my cheek lightly.

"Um . . . ," I said as Mom plopped on the couch, putting her bunny-slippered feet on the coffee table and positioning the popcorn bowl on her lap.

" 'Um' what?" Mom asked. "Are you in the mood for scary, funny or sappy?"

I sat next to her and looked her in the eye. "Where's Jake?"

Mom's hand froze as a piece of popcorn was halfway to her mouth. "What do you mean?" she asked cautiously. "Where *should* he be?"

"It's a Friday night and I've been at the skating rink for two hours," I said. "This would have been the perfect time for you to fix him a nice meal." I rolled my eyes. "Do I have to tell you everything?"

Mom smiled, but her eyes were sad. "Well, gee, as much as I appreciate you coordinating my social calendar . . ."

"I mean it, Mom. I haven't seen Jake all week, and I haven't even heard you talking to him on the phone. Now, here it is the weekend . . ."

Mom took her feet off the coffee table, put the popcorn bowl by her side and took my hands in hers. "Jake's a great guy," she said in barely a whisper. "But I don't think we're ready for a relationship right now."

I swallowed hard. "You broke up with him?"

Mom tossed her head, trying to look nonchalant. "It's not like we were a couple or anything. We'd just gone out for pizza a couple of times."

My back stiffened. "It's because of me. It's because I was such a brat the other night."

Mom stroked my cheek. "No," she said firmly. "I don't think you and I are ready to bring somebody new into our lives right now. *Either* of us."

My eyes darted as my mind raced. "We *are* ready!" I insisted. "Jake's fantastic! You're fantastic together! I don't necessarily mean that you have to elope this weekend or anything, but . . . Mom, you *dumped* him?"

Tears sprang into my eyes.

"Oh, Talia," Mom said, folding me into a hug. "I promise, it's not nearly as dramatic as you make it sound. Jake and I are still good friends. We work together, remember? He's fine. *I'm* fine."

"You're not supposed to let your stupid kid screw up your romance!" I sputtered through tears. "Who cares what I think? And by the way, in case I wasn't clear, I think he's great! I throw one little fit and he's out the door? Geez! Even baseball players get more than one strike!"

Mom squeezed me tighter. "You're giving yourself way too much credit," she said. "I do actually get a vote on whether I want to be in a relationship, you know."

"You're not voting for you," I said sadly. "You're voting for me."

Mom kissed my hair. "Honey, I have to vote for both of us. What affects one of us affects us both. We're a family. And I wouldn't have it any other way."

I pulled away and stared at her through hot tears.

"Do you like him?" I demanded.

"Oh, Talia . . ."

"Do you like him?" I repeated evenly. "Do you like Jake or not?"

"Of course I like him."

"Then call him." I hopped to my feet, grabbed the phone and put it in her hand. "Call him and tell him your bratty daughter has come to her senses. Let him pick out a movie tonight. I'm going to spend the rest of the night instant-messaging my friends in my room, so you won't hear a peep out of me. I'll be invisible. I'll even spend the night at Grandma's if you want."

"Talia!" Mom said. "Will you please take it down a notch?"

"Please call him, Mom," I beseeched her. "I'll do whatever it takes to make this right."

Mom's eyes softened. "What if it's *not* right, honey? And not because you did anything wrong, but because I really like our life just the way it is, and I really loved your dad, and I'm not sure anyone could ever take his place, and if there's even a *chance* that that's true, how unfair would it be to poor Jake to—"

"I loved Dad too," I interrupted, looking deep into her eyes. "But we can make room for somebody new in our lives. Dad would want us to." I paused, then gazed down at the phone. "Won't you please call him, Mom?"

Mom shook her head quickly. "I'm sure he's not sitting by his phone on a Friday night waiting for me to call," she said. "Besides, Talia, I'm still not sure—"

"Mom," I said, "*I'm* sure."

Her lips crept into a smile. "You don't have to worry about me, you know," she said.

"Blah, blah, blah, blah, blah," I teased. *"Call him."*

Mom bit her lower lip and pulled a lock of hair behind her ear. "I have to give this some thought," she said, as much to herself as to me. "And I'm sure he's not sitting around waiting for me to . . ." She waved her hand through the air. "I have some thinking to do, Talia. Can't we please watch a sappy movie and just chill for now?"

I studied her for a second, then sighed. "I'm not sure I'm in the mood for sappy," I said. "Scary, maybe."

"Scary it is," Mom said, reaching around me to turn on the lamp. "But only if we keep all the lights on. You know I can't handle scary in the dark."

"I'll keep you safe," I said, then turned toward her abruptly and shouted, "Boo!"

She laughed and jumped in her seat.

"Betcha you wouldn't be scared if Jake was here," I murmured, jabbing at her side.

"Betcha you better butt out of my love life," she teased, poking me back.

"Dream on," I responded. I stood up to pop a movie into the DVD player, then settled back on the couch by Mom's side. "Quit hogging the popcorn."

Talia13 has logged on.
BridgetOverTroubledWaters has logged on.

Talia13: We've got 2 talk. U know how I've spent the last couple of weeks ruining everybody's life, mostly my own?

BridgetOverTroubledWaters: So noted. Proceed with tale of woe.

Talia13: My mom broke up with Jake b-cuz of me.

BridgetOverTroubledWaters: No way! What did U do?

Talia13: Remember when they picked me up from Mer's party and I was in such a bad mood? It freaked Mom out and it probably made Jake think he would rather eat glass than have to deal w/me. I screwed everything up.

BridgetOverTroubledWaters: So do you get, like, a commission for destroying people's lives?

Talia13: HELP ME! I have 2 fix this!

BridgetOverTroubledWaters: R U sure we shouldn't leave well enough alone? Maybe Jake is an ax murderer.

Talia13: I think I've ruled that out. I Googled his name and didn't come up w/ any felonies. He's really nice. Plus, I know Mom likes him. I can tell. Then I come along and ruin everything. I am the most dispickable person in the whole world.

BridgetOverTroubledWaters: U R not a very good speller, either.

Talia13: How do U spell dispickable?

BridgetOverTroubledWaters: Let's just say evil instead.

Talia13: Will U help me?

BridgetOverTroubledWaters: OK.

Talia13: Hurry, hurry! C U soon.

Talia13 has signed off.
BridgetOverTroubledWaters has signed off.

● ● ●

Mom had left for the store by the time Bridget got to my house an hour later. I greeted her at the door with my finger holding a place in the phone book.

"Jake's phone number," I said, holding up the book.

Bridget nodded as she shut the door behind her. "Good sign. Ax murderers probably don't list their numbers in the phone book."

"I told you, I ruled out felonies." I sat on the couch and opened the book to the place I was holding. "Should I call him?"

Bridget plopped down next to me and studied the phone book intently, like she was deciphering a secret code. "That's one possibility," she murmured, still staring at the phone book.

"What are the others?" I asked.

"I don't know. . . . Hmmm. You said he had a dog. Maybe we could kidnap the dog, arrange a ransom delivery, then be waiting for him with the dog, at which point he'd be so happy to see his dog, he'd transfer his happy feelings onto us, and then—"

"Bridget!"

She pouted. "No dognapping?"

"I want to *help* my mom, not call her from jail for bail money."

"They go easy on minors, you know."

"We're not kidnapping E-bay!"

Bridget rolled her eyes. "Fine! Geez, you don't have to be so sensitive. Frankly, a phone call seems a little . . . I don't know . . . underdramatic."

"I've had way too much drama in my life lately," I muttered, picking up the phone. "Underdramatic suits me just fine."

"Wait, wait!" Bridget said, jumping up. "Let me get on the other line."

I tightened my lips. "Why?"

"So I can help you convince him to undump your mom."

"Mom dumped *him*, remember?"

"Whatever. I'm very persuasive."

I tapped my index finger against the phone. "Okay," I finally said. "You can listen in on the other line. But don't say anything unless I ask you to."

"Yeah, like that'll happen," Bridget murmured, already headed toward the kitchen to pick up the other phone.

"Bridget!" I called after her. "I mean it! This is a delicate situation."

"Just dial," she called back.

I took a deep breath. "Here goes nothing. . . ."

I pressed the numbers one by one, then held my breath and squeezed my eyes shut as I listened to his phone ring one, two, three times. Maybe he wasn't home and his answering machine would pick up. Maybe he was so devastated by Mom's rejection that he'd packed up and moved to Guadalajara in the middle of the night. Maybe he already had another girlfriend and she was standing next to him, ready to laugh her head off. Maybe—

"Hello?"

I gulped. "Uh . . ."

"Hello?" Jake repeated, this time sounding annoyed.

"Yeah . . . ," I said quickly. "Um . . . Jake?"

"Yes, this is Jake. Who am I speaking to?"

Dead silence.

"It's Talia," Bridget blurted from her extension.

I hissed in Bridget's general direction.

"Talia?" Jake repeated, his voice softening.

Dead silence.

"Yes, Talia," Bridget said.

"Bridget!" I moaned.

More silence. "What's going on?" Jake asked slowly.

"Um . . . ," I said.

"I see I'm going to have to take matters into my own hands," Bridget said briskly. "Jake, we've never met, but I'm Talia's best friend, Bridget. Perhaps she's spoken of me? I'm the one she's spent the last couple of weeks treating like a cretin? Right, that's me. Well, here's the thing—"

"Is this some sort of a put-on?" Jake asked, his voice a mixture of curiosity and irritation.

"No, no put-on," Bridget continued. "Talia wanted to talk to you, but for some reason, she's been rendered mute all of a sudden, and I'm in her kitchen on the other line, so—"

"Bridget, please!" I sputtered. But I didn't know what to say after that, so more silence followed.

"O-*kay*," Bridget said. "Jake, don't judge Talia by her conversational skills. She's got many other nice qualities."

"This *is* a put-on," Jake said evenly.

"No!" I blurted. "It's not a put-on. Jake, I have to say this fast, or I'll lose my nerve. My mom would kill me if she knew I was calling you, but you need to know that the only reason she broke up with you is that I was being such a—"

"Cretin," Bridget offered.

"Okay, cretin," I said, "but here's the thing: she really likes you."

I held my breath for a second, then blew it out like air escaping from a popped balloon.

"Your mom doesn't know you're calling me?" he asked.

"That would be a no," Bridget said. "You *do* like her, right?"

Jake cleared his throat. "Can I plead the Fifth until I've had a chance to talk to her?"

"Talk is highly overrated," Bridget said. "It's time for action. Come to dinner tonight. Talia and I are cooking."

"We—wha-a-a?" I stammered.

"We'll cook, then get out of your way and let you two have some alone time."

"Bridget!" I shrieked. "We can't cook!"

"Can you come?" she asked Jake.

Jake paused, then said, "I really need to talk to your mom first, Talia."

"So talk! Talk when you come to dinner tonight," Bridget said.

"Hmmmm...," he responded. "I guess there'll be plenty of time for talk, since you two can't cook."

"We'll improvise," Bridget said.

"What if Chelsea doesn't want me to come over?" Jake asked.

"Talia," Bridget responded, "have you ever in your whole life invited a friend over that your mom kicked out?"

"Never," I replied.

"I'm guessing Talia's guests have never included her mother's friends," Jake murmured. "Okay, here's the deal: I have to cover a football game later today for work. So *if* the game doesn't end too late, and *if* Chelsea knows I'm coming and doesn't mind, and *if* she doesn't decide to give up her scheming daughter for adoption, and *if* you two don't set the kitchen on fire . . . then I'll come."

"You drive a hard bargain," Bridget said. "But Mrs. Farrow can't know you're coming. She might put the ol' ix-nay on our plan."

"Yeah, that's something I'd kinda like to anticipate in advance," Jake said. "Rejection isn't everything it's cracked up to be."

"She won't reject you," I said. "She really, really likes you, Jake."

He sighed. "The game should be over by seven. I'll *casually* drop by your house when it's over—'Hi, Chels, just happened to be in the neighborhood'—then try not to look too pathetic if this little plan implodes."

"Works for us!" Bridget said.

"Did I mention I like homemade manicotti?" he said.

"Don't push it," Bridget replied.

I'd been watching from the window, and as soon as I saw Mom pulling into the driveway, Bridget and I ran out to greet her.

"Will you take us to the mall?" I asked her as she unloaded groceries from the trunk.

"Please?" Bridget said. "I've been dying to go. I heard Threads is having a sale."

Mom cocked her head skeptically. "Since when are you interested in Threads?" she asked Bridget, handing us bags as she pulled them from the trunk.

"Oh, I've started a registry there," Bridget said. "My birthday's not until January, but you never know when people might want to buy me a gift. I think Armistice Day is coming up."

Mom smiled and tousled Bridget's hair. "I'm so glad you made up with Talia," she said. "I've missed you."

"Then take us to the mall and spend all day with her!" I said.

Bridget and I weren't convinced that Jake wouldn't try to call Mom, and we didn't want to take any chances. We'd keep her out of the house all afternoon, and I'd slip into her purse when she wasn't looking to turn off her cell phone.

"Mall! Mall! Mall! Mall!" Bridget chanted.

"Well," Mom said. "Okay. Let's unload the groceries and I'll take my material girls shopping."

• • •

By the time we got home almost four hours later, Bridget and I realized we had slightly over an hour to cook a romantic dinner for two, minus any skills or ingredients to speak of.

We had talked Mom into buying some froufrou soaps and lotions at the mall, so we insisted she go take a long, hot bath and try them out.

"You girls are acting awfully strange today," she said, but she didn't need much coaxing.

We scooted her off to the bathroom, then huddled in the kitchen to plot our next move.

"Do you know how to make manicotti?" Bridget asked in a hushed voice.

"Of course I don't know how to make manicotti!"

"Shhh!"

"I don't even know what manicotti is," I said grumpily, lowering my voice to a whisper.

"Well, we have to come up with something," Bridget

said, glancing nervously around the room as if a gourmet dinner might magically materialize.

"It was your bright idea to cook," I reminded her, furrowing my brow. "I don't even make my own peanut-butter-and-jelly sandwiches."

"It's high time you learned," Bridget said, walking over to the pantry and burying her head inside.

I started absently opening cupboards, drawers and refrigerator crispers. Every once in a while, I'd pull out a spatula or a can of shortening, having no idea how they might fit into our meal.

"Bridget, the only thing I know how to use in the kitchen is the phone," I moaned. "Can we just order pizza?"

"Nope. We said we were cooking, and we're cooking."

By now, the kitchen counters were filling with boxes, jars and cans, none of which looked like they could combine to make a meal, but, really, what did I know? Bridget and I bustled about for the next forty minutes, opening cans, stirring pots, clattering pans, mixing ingredients and setting a table for two in the dining room. I stuck a couple of tapered candles in candlesticks, but they kept tilting, so Bridget took the gum from her mouth, divided it in two and spread it around the base of each candle.

"I'm a genius! It works!" she said with her hands on her hips as we surveyed the results.

"It looks a little messy," I said skeptically. "And besides, how's Mom going to get the gum off the candlesticks?"

"You reuse candlesticks?" she said. "Well, the gum will be there to help her keep the next set of candles in place."

We jumped with a start as we heard Mom's bedroom

door open down the hall. "Do I smell something burning?" she called.

"Bridget! The cornflakes!" I said, and Bridget rushed to check her cornflakes on the stove, stirring them and lowering the heat.

"It's five till seven," Bridget said, her hands fluttering as she ran back into the dining room. "Go tell your mom to put on a ball gown or something."

We glanced up to see Mom padding down the hallway toward the dining room, smoothing her damp, shampoo-scented hair.

"Mom!" I said, surveying her flannel pajama pants, Myrtle Beach sweatshirt and bunny slippers.

"*What,*" she said, furrowing her brow as she came closer, "is going on?"

Bridget and I beamed proudly. "We cooked dinner," I said.

"*You?* Cooked *dinner?* You cooked *dinner? You?*" Mom peered over our shoulders into the kitchen. "What in the world . . . ?" Her eyes darted to the table. "Candlelight? We're eating by candlelight?"

"Not exactly us," I said, picking a piece of lint off Mom's sweatshirt. "Mom, you have to change."

"Something flouncy," Bridget instructed. "Girly and flouncy. Like a party dress."

Mom's jaw tightened. "It's time," she said in her calm-on-the-verge-of-hysterical tone, "for you two to tell me what's going on."

The doorbell rang.

"What," Mom repeated through gritted teeth, "is going on?"

"I'll get it!" Bridget said cheerfully, headed toward the front door.

"Don't be mad," I beseeched Mom.

Her eyes widened.

We heard the front door shut. Bridget rejoined us in the dining room. A couple of seconds later, Jake followed her into the room carrying a handful of wildflowers. He smiled sheepishly at Mom, who looked too stunned to speak.

"Hi, Chels," he said. "I was covering a ball game nearby, so I was kind of in the neighborhood, and I thought I'd . . . oh, never mind."

Mom's eyes darted from the flowers to the candles to the kitchen, then back to the flowers. She opened her mouth to speak, but squeezed her eyes shut and shook her head instead.

"We cooked you guys dinner!" Bridget said triumphantly.

"Uh, us?" Mom stammered, waving her finger back and forth from Jake to herself.

"Right," Bridget said. "It's Saturday night, and Talia and I thought, *How can we keep the old folks out of our hair while we try out explosive devices in the garage?*"

"So you knew about this," Mom said slowly to Jake.

He shrugged. "They called me a few hours ago. I tried to call you to make sure it was okay that I stopped by, but—"

"Details, details!" Bridget said quickly, waving her hand through the air. "What does it matter who called who, or when, or why? You're here, Jake's here, the table is set, the candles are lit, the flowers are beautiful, dinner's on the stove—"

"So to speak . . . ," Mom murmured, peering anxiously into the kitchen.

Bridget took the flowers from Jake, handed them to me, then cleared her throat dramatically. "Sir and madam," she intoned, "your evening will begin with appetizers in the drawing room."

"The drawing room," Mom repeated numbly.

Bridget took each of them by the arm and walked them toward the living room. I scanned a kitchen cabinet for a vase, settled for a mason jar, filled it with water, put the flowers inside and placed it on the dining room table.

"Champagne! We need champagne!" Bridget whispered, rushing back into the dining room.

"Champagne? Oh, sure. We keep it around all the time," I said. "Are you crazy? We don't have champagne!"

"Wine?"

I shrugged. "I don't know. I don't think so."

Bridget rolled her eyes. "You people are hopeless! Oh, well. I saw some apple juice in the refrigerator. Open it and I'll get a couple of wine glasses from the china cabinet."

I grabbed the apple juice, which she poured into crystal goblets. She frowned, then retrieved some cinnamon-flavored sprinkles. She shook the sprinkles into the goblets and gave a satisfied nod.

"Looks elegant," she said, then whisked the glasses into the living room.

"Are they sitting close to each other?" I whispered when she came back into the kitchen.

"They're on the same couch, but considering that your mom's wearing bunny slippers, I'm not sure how much romance we can pull off," Bridget said. "Never mind. Help me with these appetizers."

I glanced quizzically around the kitchen. "Which are the appetizers?"

Bridget walked over to the stove, stirring the cornflakes she'd mixed with peanut butter and marshmallow cream.

"Get a serving tray," she instructed.

I grabbed one from the china cabinet, brought it to the stove, and helped Bridget pluck pinches of the mixture from the pot onto the tray.

"They look . . . goopy," I said.

"We'll bring them napkins."

We filled the tray, grabbed napkins and carried our "appetizers" into the "drawing room." Mom and Jake were peering curiously into their apple juice goblets as we walked in.

"Sir? Madam?" Bridget said, presenting the tray to them as I handed them napkins.

"Mmmmmm," Jake said. "What might these be?"

"Buttercream Crunch Balls," Bridget responded in her high-society accent.

Jake took a small bite and winced. "Nice and sweet," he said, then let his sticky fingers linger in the air.

"Girls," Mom said, holding her appetizer right outside her lips, "as adorable as this all is, in its own highly disturbing, juvenile-delinquent kind of way, what were you thinking when—"

"When we let you wear those bunny slippers?" Bridget said. "I don't know. We were clearly insane. Might I take this opportunity to replace them with more appropriate footwear, madam? Some bejeweled high heels, perhaps?"

Mom snickered. "I'll stick with the slippers."

Bridget bowed with a flourish. "In that case, madam, we shall retreat to the food-service quarters, where we will commence serving your meal."

"You know, I'm getting awfully full on these appetizers and this . . . sediment-speckled juice," Jake said. "I'm not sure how much more fine dining I can take."

Mom wrinkled her nose. "What exactly might the main course be?" she asked.

"Jake requested manicotti, and we didn't know how to make that," Bridget answered.

"We weren't even sure what it was," I added.

"So we made canimotti instead," Bridget said.

Mom raised an eyebrow. "What's canimotti?"

"Our own creation," I explained proudly. "Lots of cans mixed together."

"Cans of what?" Mom asked.

I bit my bottom lip. "Um, just stuff we could find. There was some chicken noodle soup, some green beans—"

"Some water chestnuts," Bridget added.

Jake popped the rest of his Buttercream Crunch Ball into his mouth and stood up. "Tragically, I'm allergic to canimotti," he said. "Makes my throat muscles snap shut like a crocodile snout. It's a rare yet deadly allergy, and it would seem unbearably rude to drop dead in your drawing room, or your dining quarters or wherever, so . . ."

"So what do you suggest?" Mom said, grinning at him.

"We can't take you anywhere in your bunny slippers,"

he said, giving Mom a once-over and making her giggle, "so I suggest . . . ordering in pizza?"

"Pizza!" I cheered, jumping up and down. "That was my idea in the first place!"

"Can you guys at least eat our dessert?" Bridget said with a pout.

"If you guys mixed any two ingredients together, not a chance," Jake said.

"We have ice cream," Mom volunteered, raising her hand.

"Pizza and ice cream!" I cheered, and this time, Bridget joined me jumping up and down.

"Pizza and ice cream it is," Mom said.

"And Buttercream Crunch Balls," Bridget added. "You can't forget our Buttercream Crunch Balls."

Jake inhaled slowly with a smile. "This," he said appreciatively, "is shaping up to be one killer evening."

● ● ●

I held my ear against my bedroom door. "They're laughing," I reported to Bridget.

We'd polished off our pizza, played a few rounds of charades, dumped the canimotti down the garbage disposal and washed the dishes before heading off to my room for the night, leaving Mom and Jake alone in the living room. They were supposedly watching a movie, but they were doing more talking than anything, Mom's voice sounding like crystal tinkling and Jake's sounding like a friendly bear.

"Jake's awesome," Bridget said, plumping the pillows on my bed and flipping channels with the remote control.

"Yeah, he's pretty cool. I think he really likes my mom."

"Uh, duh. Like he'd be playing charades with two kids on a Saturday night unless he was totally in love."

"I didn't say anything about *love*," I said with a grin, plopping on the bed beside her and propping up on my elbows.

"It's love. Better get used to it," Bridget said.

"What do you know about love?" I asked playfully.

"I know Jake is in it. And so is your mom."

Tap, tap, tap.

Mom cracked open my door and peeked inside. "You girls doing okay?" she asked.

"We're fine, Mom. Get back to Jake."

"Yeah, speaking of Jake," she said, walking in, "if you two ever spring a surprise date on me again, I'll shave your heads in the middle of the night."

"Are you having fun?" Bridget asked with sparkling eyes.

"That's beside the point. The point is . . . Oh, okay, fine: yes, I'm having fun."

"You're blushing, Mom!"

"Am not," she insisted, sitting between us on the bed.

"Are too. Jake always makes you blush."

"No more dumping him," Bridget scolded her playfully. "I don't know how many more gourmet meals I can manage. Although, if I say so myself, I thought the Buttercream Crunch Balls were delicious."

"They were exquisite," Mom said, putting an arm around each of us and squeezing us tightly. "You girls are really something. But a little warning next time so I can—

oh, I don't know—maybe smudge on a little makeup before a date?"

"You look prettier without it," I said, and she really did. Her cheeks were glowing.

I had to hand it to Jake: he could really make Mom's cheeks glow.

30

"You'll never believe what happened Saturday," Mom said to Chad during her Monday-morning *Up and At 'Em*. Our fingers dangled together as we watched the tape that evening.

"I give up," Chad said.

"Talia cooked me dinner."

"And the house is still standing?"

Mom grinned. "Actually, the dinner she cooked never made it onto the table. She and her best friend kind of bit off more than they could chew."

The audience groaned good-naturedly.

"But it's the thought that counts, right?" Mom continued. "Another first . . . first tooth, first step, first word, first sleepover, first day of school . . . now her first dinner."

"The dinner that you didn't actually eat," Chad said.

"You don't always appreciate the significance of mile-stones as they're happening," Mom said with an amused look in her eyes. "For instance, I didn't appreciate the significance of the first time Talia changed the radio station in the car. Little did I know that from that point forward her musical preferences would rule whenever we were in the car. And the first time she spent her allowance on a CD? She never pulled her Barbies out from under her bed again after that. It's only in looking back that you realize these are milestones, you know? So I tried not to miss the significance of her first dinner."

"The dinner no one actually ate," Chad repeated, making the audience laugh.

"I don't know how to describe it, but something about realizing she could operate major appliances without my supervision made my heart melt."

"Are you ready to turn over the range to her for good?" Chad asked.

Mom wrinkled her nose. "Nah. But there's that subtle transition as you're raising kids when you realize you're not always going to be the one taking care of them. At a certain point, they start returning the favor."

Her eyes misted.

"You're getting weepy about the dinner that no one actually ate," Chad wisecracked.

"Yeah," Mom said. "I guess I am."

"Reporting live from Crossroads Middle School, this is Talia Farrow with Talia Talk.

"My mom's already broken the news on her show, but just to make sure everyone hears my side . . . First, let's get the embarrassing part out of the way right up front: I cooked my first meal Saturday, and it ended up in the garbage disposal. It was Saturday night, and my BFF and I decided to cook dinner for my mom and her friend. Long story. We thought, *How hard could it be? Our moms whip up our dinners every day, and we barely even notice what they're doing. Must be a breeze, right?*

"Not really. I learned Saturday night that cooking isn't nearly as easy as it looks. Lots of things are involved: getting the right ingredients, having the right tools, knowing how to use them, knowing how to mix the ingredients together, knowing how long to cook them. It's a long list, and my BFF and I got nearly every step wrong.

"So if cooking is so much tougher than it looks, it makes me wonder what else my mom does that is harder than it seems. For instance, she goes to work every day, even when she doesn't feel like it. She buys me stuff, even if it means she has to go without. She pays all the bills. She spends her free time taking care of me and running me around.

"And she does it all herself. My dad died when I was little, so Mom doesn't get much of a break. My grandparents are great, and we have lots of awesome friends, but I'm sure my mom has it tough sometimes. Yet she never makes it *seem* tough, which is why I thought cooking would be easier than it turned out to be. She makes hard things look easy. So even though she totally embarrasses me on her show, I hope she'll start putting herself first every once in a while instead of always worrying about me.

"That doesn't mean she gets a pass for all the embarrassing things she's said about me on her show over the years.

"But it might mean she doesn't have to be the only cook in the kitchen.

"We'll have to stick with simple recipes—maybe hot dogs and canned beans until I get the hang of things—but I'm thinking we'll make a pretty good team.

"Signing off for now, this is Talia Farrow for the Crossroads Oddcast."

One Year Later . . .

"Oooh, end piece, end piece!"

The lady cutting the cake looked annoyed but gave Bridget an end piece anyhow.

"Have you tried the shrimp? They're delicious," we overheard one guest tell another as they circled the buffet. "And I don't know what these crunchy little things are, but they're very good."

"They're Buttercream Crunch Balls," Mom called from a few feet over, winking at Bridget and me.

Bridget smiled at her, then adjusted the spaghetti strap of her teal junior bridesmaid's dress. "Shouldn't we get royalties for our recipe?" she asked me.

"You get royalties for songs, not recipes."

The disc jockey started playing "Brown-Eyed Girl." "Speaking of songs," I told Bridget, swaying to the beat, "I love this one."

"In that case," a voice behind me said, "may I have this dance?"

I turned around and smiled at Jake. "I still can't get used to you in a monkey suit," I told him.

"You won't have to. You'll never see me in one again after today, I promise." He took my hand, spread our arms wide and gave me a gentle tug closer to the dance floor.

"I'm a terrible dancer," I confessed as he guided my moves with the hand he held behind my back.

"I know, but I think it's a rule that the groom has to dance with the maid of honor," he said. "Try to look presentable, will ya?"

I stuck out my tongue and crossed my eyes. He opened our embrace with a little jerk and twirled me around, making me squeal.

"I hear your Buttercream Crunch Balls are a big hit," he said as he folded me back in.

"Duh," I said. "Bridget says we should charge for letting people use the recipe."

"Fair enough," Jake said. "But you're the one who gets sued if anyone goes into insulin shock."

"Are we saving a piece of wedding cake for E-bay?" I asked.

"If you say so. But you get to clean up after him in the morning."

"You think he'll miss you and Mom while you're on your honeymoon?"

"Nah. You and your grandparents will take good care of him. Just show him my picture a couple of times a day."

Mom and Grandpa glided past us on the dance floor; then Grandpa dipped her under my nose, making us both laugh.

"Can your grandpa cut a rug or what?" Grandpa said.

"He sure can," Jake told me. "I should be dancing with him."

"Oh, that can be arranged," I teased. Mom and I opened our arms and joined hands, and soon all four of us were dancing in a circle.

"Hey, what about me?" Grandma called, shimmying over to the dance floor.

"And me!" Bridget called, rushing to my side and flapping her arms like wings. The deejay noticed her and changed the music to the "Chicken Dance."

"Oh, honey, it's our song!" Mom told Jake, and we all started flapping around, dissolving into giggles.

"Smile!" Ben and Shelley called from a few feet over, and we waved into the camcorder.

I couldn't help but notice how elegant Mom looked, even doing the Chicken Dance. But what I noticed most of all was the glow in her cheeks.

I had to hand it to Jake: he really could make Mom's cheeks glow.

CHRISTINE HURLEY DERISO, author of *Do-Over* and *The Right-Under Club,* lives in South Carolina with her husband, Graham, and their children, Greg and Julianne. Visit her at www.christinehurleyderiso.com.